MISTAKEN

SHOTGUN FALLS SHIFTERS

AVA BENTON

LIBBY BERNARD

1

W hat a night.

Esme Redferne stood over her friend's bed, drawing a blanket across the thin, trembling body. Amy shivered even in sleep, even after taking the potion Esme had put together to calm her understandably frayed nerves and the physical pain she'd endured.

It was the psychological pain that haunted Amy now, no matter the potion she drank. Magic could ease things, smooth the rough edges, but it couldn't erase unless a witch was willing to chance wiping out other memories. It was too dangerous to make Amy forget. She could only take the edge off.

Esme'd learned from experience. Everybody had something they wanted to forget.

She could feel it, could almost taste it in the air. It had a bitter quality, that pain, swirling so thick around the bed in which Amy slept and dreamed her painful dreams now that she was home and safe. Memories, more like, fresh and vivid only hours after the attack which brought her to Esme's door.

Not many things could coax the witch from her home, her haven. It was easier to keep away from the world. Safer. Even healthier at times. So much energy in the air, so much pain and anger and sorrow and need in the humans populating Shotgun Falls and the world at large. It was too much to bear after only a little while. Like sticking a toe into an ice-cold lake, knowing the rest of the water would be no warmer. A single toe was enough.

That would be enough were it not for the new dangers. Terrible, wicked, painful dangers like what Amy had suffered along with the friends she'd been out with that night. The Goddess must've been guiding her through the woods after coming to, leading her to Esme's cabin.

Amy shivered. A single, violent spasm which brought Esme's attention back to her, and to the energy she herself poured into the room by attempting to imagine what her fellow witches had suffered. The sort of hatred and evil required to torture innocent women the way Amy described Esme drove her home and tucked her into bed.

Esme bent over her, running a gentle hand over Amy's damp hair and sending as much calming energy as possible. She'd showered after arriving at the cabin, something Esme had encouraged her to do. There were wounds that needed cleaning, for one thing, not to mention the dirt and twigs clinging to her hair, skin, clothes.

While the shower ran, Esme had snipped herbs from the pots around her kitchen, then used her mortar and pestle to grind them into a poultice for the cuts and scrapes. Marshmallow for inflammation, slippery elm bark. She mixed them together before adding the juice from an aloe stem to create a paste while setting the intention behind the poultice, sending some of her magic into it. *Goddess, grant healing to she who wears this.*

While she'd applied them to Amy's wounds—the raw skin around her wrist and ankles, the bites to her shoulders and legs—her friend had explained how the wounds came to be. Not that Esme needed much explanation. There were already plenty of rumors in their world, among their kind. Witches needed to be more careful than ever.

"We went to the bar. Full Moon." Of course. It

was a bar for supernaturals, the most popular one in the state. Also one of the only ones where shifter shenanigans were frowned upon, which probably made it as popular as it was. Everyone wanted to have a good time without wolves and bears, and who knew what else throwing down and baring their fangs. Some supernaturals liked it that way, liked being on-edge. It added excitement and danger to what could otherwise be a typical night out. Amy didn't feel that way, though she wasn't as reclusive as Esme, either.

"What happened there?" Esme had wrapped Amy's wrists in gauze after applying the paste, using as gentle a touch as possible. Even then, Amy had winced more than once.

"Nothing I was aware of. It was me, Moira, Rachel, and Cassie. We were having fun, minding our own business, when..."

"When?"

"I don't know, exactly. There were shifters there for sure. A couple of packs, sort of keeping to their respective ends of the bar. I went to the bathroom, and when I came back, there were drinks for all of us. I guessed one of the girls had gone over to order them."

Esme's gut tightened at the thought of it.

"I drank it, and then... I don't know." Amy had shrugged, eyes on the floor. Ashamed. Maybe angry with herself for not being more careful. "The next thing I knew, I was in the woods. We all were, the four of us. Sitting propped against trees with our ankles bound."

She'd lifted her left wrist, the one so raw and angry looking. "And we were wearing bracelets that didn't belong to us."

It took every ounce of control to keep from gasping, from gripping Amy's wounded wrist too hard. "Bracelets? What kind?"

"I don't know. Thick links. I couldn't figure out the kind of metal—that was the weirdest part. I should've been able to tell the sort of materials used if they were natural. From the earth. This? I couldn't get a read on any of it. Neither could the other girls."

She'd finished in a whisper. "We couldn't use our powers. They took our powers."

"They did what?" The lights flickered thanks to the sudden surge of Esme's energy. She could feel it crackling down to the ends of her short, flaming red hair. It couldn't be. Not again.

"I think it was the bracelets. They sort of burned whenever we tried to do anything. You know, like using our abilities to loosen the ropes on our ankles. They were so tight, my feet were turning numb. Moira tried to light the area around us using her aura, but she could hardly flicker." Some witches were experts at light work the way Esme specialized in reading and manipulating energy, emotions. Moira was one of them—except when she wore a strange bracelet that suppressed her powers.

"What happened next?" By then, nothing could've kept Esme from hearing the rest, even if it meant dredging everything up for Amy. Keeping it bottled up wouldn't have done her any good, though, something Esme reminded herself when the pain in her friend's eyes left her wondering whether going over it was a good idea.

"They were there. A pack of shifters. They must've been waiting and watching to see if we'd be able to free ourselves. We did, but there was no removing the bracelets. No clasp we could find, too tight to go over our hands. They finally called out to us, told us we were playing hide and seek."

She'd wrapped her arms around her trembling body while her voice rose in pitch until it was barely a squeak. "They told us to run. So we ran. In the dark, in the cold. I can still hear them behind us, right behind us, crashing through the brush and laughing the entire way. Calling out to us. Howling, even."

A tear rolled down her cheek. "It was worse than the worst nightmare you can imagine. We were still woozy from whatever they gave us at the bar to knock us out. Disoriented. We had no idea where we were. All I knew was, I couldn't let them catch me." Another tear. "But they did."

"And they bit you."

"Bit us, beat us." The evidence of that was all over Amy's body, including a bruise that spanned her back from side to side. Like somebody had brought a limb down across it. Esme had applied ointment to that, something to ease the pain and promote healing. "When they were finished, they dumped our bodies in a dried-up creek, half over-grown. They probably thought they killed us."

"But they didn't. You're too strong for that."

Esme's encouragement had gone unnoticed.

"They took off the bracelets, too."

"Of course they did." How did they manage, though? None of the girls were conscious by the time the night's evil festivities had ended, so Amy had no way of knowing. She'd also not managed to get a look at any of the shifters who'd eventually caught up to and brutally beaten the witches. It was too dark, and she was too scared. And hurting so much.

Esme left her with fresh poultice and more of the tincture she'd put in Amy's tea to help her sleep, along with a note instructing her how to use both. Not all witches were as skilled at herbal remedies as she was, so it wouldn't pay to take chances and assume she knew the correct dosage. The worst of the wounds would be healed by morning, but the mental toll? Who knew?

All the way home, the question of who did it plagued Esme. It continued to tug at her consciousness as she walked into her cabin, quiet and calm as she'd left it. Tonight had only solidified the choice she'd made to withdraw from society. If nobody wanted to protect witches, they'd have to protect themselves. Maybe Amy and the other girls would be more careful from then on out.

She went to the sink and washed her tools under the light hanging in front of the window, her heart blazing the entire time. Burning so hot, she wondered if it might scorch her from the inside out.

Because there was only one shifter cruel enough to pull a stunt like the one Amy had described. Only one who hated witches the way someone would have to if they were going to torture a group of them. Chasing them down like animals, like prey.

Imagine. She thought she'd loved him once. A long time ago. It was his father's influence, she had no doubt, though Derek was a full-grown shifter. His father might have been pack alpha, and Jordan never let an opportunity pass without reminding everyone how much he hated witches, but Derek didn't have to follow along. He was old enough to make his own choices.

What had pushed him over the edge? Esme had theories. They involved her.

Her footsteps were the only sound in the house as she left the kitchen in favor of going to her room. A small room, decorated with probably too many plants and stuffed with books. They sat in stacks on the nightstand, on the floor, lined up on the windowsills, and of course, packed into a pair of bookcases. There were even a few random strays underneath the bed, which was where she reached to pull out the box she hadn't opened since the breakup. Since Jordan's hatred of witches—and his son's inability to think for himself—had come between them.

She'd given him an ultimatum. It wasn't her style, never had been. She didn't believe in forcing people into doing things, not even with her powers. It was easy to manipulate a person's emotions, their mental state. Even shifters, though humans were much easier. Most of them didn't believe witchcraft existed in the first place, so they had fewer walls built up around their minds to block outside interference.

With Derek, though, there was no question he'd have to make a decision and stick to it. Either stand up to his father's hatred and bigotry or say goodbye.

She found the picture, the only picture she'd kept. Locked in a box where she couldn't see it, but tucked under her bed. What did that mean? Was there some deeper psychological twistiness there? Staring at it, at the once-happy couple—they were so young, so naïve, standing with their arms around each other and the Rockies behind them—she could almost hear their last conversation before everything fell apart.

"I can't see a future for us if you keep agreeing with your father."

"But I don't. Not about you, especially." He imagined that would soothe her somehow, that she would feel better and be contented to let things go along the way they always had. Yet when he reached for her, she pulled away.

"What about my friends? My family? What makes them so different from me?" He turned away from her, scoffing and snickering. Crushing her heart.

"It's not the same. I know you. I love you. Why isn't that enough?"

She took him by the shoulder and yanked him around. If it wasn't for the element of surprise, there was no way she could've moved him or any fully grown shifter without her magic. *"How do I know you won't change your mind? We could have a fight, or you could get jealous the way you sometimes do, and who knows where that would leave me? You'd write me off as just another one of those filthy, lying witches."*

"That isn't true." There was another reaction behind his eyes. The light left them. The space around him went cold enough to raise goosebumps on her arms. Didn't he know better than to lie to her? She was a walking, talking lie detector.

Not that he was lying. He could well have believed the words he spoke. But there was doubt, too. Uncertainty.

At the time, she'd believed that was the worst of it. That he couldn't hurt her any more deeply than he already had with his flippancy, his stubborn determination not to take her seriously.

She'd been so wrong.

He had to be behind the torture that night. He and his friends, none of whom Esme had ever trusted. Nasty, cruel, crude. They'd smile to her face, but their energy always told a different story. It took no imagination to picture them hunting witches through the woods before beating them half to death.

Worst of all was suspecting he'd done this because of her. She had turned him completely against witches, had pushed him over the edge. He was so far gone now, the edge was nowhere in sight. He wanted vengeance. Blood.

And he wanted her to know. *Look what you made me do, Esme.*

Her hand shook, making the image before her shake with it. She steadied herself, stared down at the almost violet eyes she had once loved looking into. What she was about to do wasn't something she took lightly, but it was the only way. He had to pay. They all did.

It didn't take long to set things up. A circle of salt, a candle in the center which she lit before whispering a prayer to the Goddess. She sat cross-legged on the floor before picking up the photo again and tearing it in two down the middle. Separating them for good.

"I curse you." Her voice was barely a whisper at first, but it grew stronger with every word. "I curse you and all who participated in hunting Amy, Moira, Rachel, and Cassie this night. You will know nothing but agony from this night forward. You will know nothing but pain each time you attempt to shift into your wolf form. The pain will tear your mind to pieces and feel like fire in your veins. You will suffer a hundredfold the torment you delivered to the innocent."

One last look at Derek's bright smile before holding the corner of the image to the candle's flame. It leapt to greater life, almost lighting the entire living room. "I call upon the Goddess to make this so." She watched the fire overtake Derek's image. Finally, there was nothing to do but drop it into the shallow bowl beside the candle, where the paper bubbled and curled.

Somewhere in the night, a wolf howled.

2

What a night.

There was nothing like hunting with the pack during a full moon. All of them together, working as one. Moving in sync after so many years of running through the same familiar woods, where Micah knew every rock and tree by heart.

Best of all, Ezra was with them. His absence had been a sore spot for Micah, like the missing piece of a puzzle. Everything had felt off when he was away from the pack, hiding himself thanks to a witch's curse that had left him and his wolf separated for months. For a while, he thought the wolf was gone for good. That he'd have to face the rest of his life with half of himself missing.

There was nothing like the freedom of running with the pack under the full moon. He was truly himself—they all were, letting their wolves take over and do as wolves had done since the dawn of time. Refreshing the connection to the woods, to each other, to the moon itself. Corny? Maybe. But there was no shaking the sense of it as dawn broke, and they gathered around their vehicles, now walking on two legs again.

"I've missed this." Ezra shook out his rumpled clothes, wearing a look of relief and satisfaction shared by the rest of the pack. "I know I said that last moon, but it still stands."

"So long as Hope doesn't mind you being away all night." Xavier winked Micah's way. "Not many women would be okay with their man heading out and leaving the other side of the bed cold."

"Don't worry. Hope is plenty satisfied with the way things are." They left it there, laughing and joking the way they always did when coming down from the high of a stag hunt.

Micah didn't have a woman waiting at home for him, but it was just as well. There was nothing he wanted more than a shower before falling into bed and sleeping all day.

Until a foreign scent touched the air.

His head snapped up, and he sniffed, the wolf inside him trying to locate the direction the scent originated from. Others followed suit, peering into the woods surrounding the clearing where they'd parked. Another shifter, undoubtedly, but not one of their own.

A moment later, the sound of an engine, the crunch of tires rolling over the ground. A Range Rover pulled into view, and the driver wasted no time, gunning the engine once he caught sight of the pack. Micah tensed, prepared to dart out of the way if the car didn't slow.

It did, just in time to keep from crashing into the parked vehicles. They waited, all of them ready to fight—Micah could feel it, could hear his tired wolf rousing himself in preparation. The driver almost fell out from behind the wheel, wild-eyed. "You have to come. You have to see what's happening."

It was a member of the pack from over in Cedar Woods. Not exactly rivals to the Shotgun Falls pack, but they weren't friends, either. Since when did any of them obey orders from Jordan Greystone or any of his members?

Adam, the Shotgun Falls pack alpha, stepped forward, arms folded, clearly sizing up the messenger. "What is it?"

"Trouble with the pack. Big trouble. Jordan told me to bring your alpha. I think he wants to warn you."

"Warn us of what?" Micah looked around and found everybody else as confused as he was.

"You'll have to come and see. Jordan's complex, the big house up in Cedar Woods. You familiar with it?"

Adam nodded. "Sure. I don't trust your alpha, though, and he knows that."

"It's not my problem, either way." He ran a hand over hair which Micah now noticed was dampening worse every second. He was sweating bullets. "Believe me. You want to know about this. Or else you might end up going through the same thing some of us are going through right now."

Ezra glanced at Adam. "Maybe we should go."

"We?" Adam snickered. "When did this turn into we?"

Micah saw the point. "We're not going to send you alone." Besides, he wanted to see this for himself. Whatever was going on, it was bad enough for a rival pack to reach out. Bad enough for this stranger to sweat through his clothes.

Adam saw he was outnumbered. "Fine. Let's go." The others filtered away, reluctant, but Ezra promised to reach out with any news. They took his truck, following Jordan's messenger through Shotgun Falls and further out, to the foot of the mountains surrounding the valley in which Shotgun Falls nestled.

"It's like a fortress." Ezra shook his head in wonder, though there was disapproval in his voice. "Why does he need the walls and fences?"

"Because he doesn't have many friends." Adam snickered as he turned the truck at the gate, where a pair of guards stared in suspicion. They didn't try to stop the visitors, though, so their presence had been forewarned.

"What do you think is happening? What could be this important?" Micah didn't expect an answer, and he didn't get one. All he wanted was a shower and a pillow under his head, but instead, he could be strolling into a trap. His wolf was at the ready, prepared to fight, though human reasoning reminded him Jordan's pack would also have hunted in the light of the moon. They'd be sated, tired. So he hoped, anyway.

The messenger hardly waited for them to follow him out of the truck, darting up the wide stairs leading to a pair of massive wooden doors. He left the door open and kept moving across a tiled foyer, to a door in the wall beneath a sweeping staircase. They were supposed to follow him to the basement?

"Something's wrong here." Not that Ezra needed to announce it. The hair at the base of Micah's neck stood up straight, and his wolf growled in his head, but they followed Adam's lead. At that point, curiosity was stronger than apprehension. They jogged down a set of stone stairs and through a low doorway leading to a wide, deep basement that could've been used as a ballroom in earlier times.

Just then, there was no party going on.

"What the…" Micah fell back a step once he got a look at the chaos inside the room. It was like a punch in the gut, seeing so many of his kind in various degrees of pain.

One thing was for sure: they were in legitimate agony, all of them. No other word could describe it.

He recognized Derek, Jordan's son, right off. They crossed paths in town from time to time, staying clear of each other when it happened. The tall, powerful shifter with his coal-black hair, eyes that were almost purple. Girls loved those eyes of his.

Now, his eyes were bloodshot, swimming with tears. "What is this?" His voice was the bloodcurdling cry of someone in the throes of death, or something that felt like it. He doubled over, clutching his head in both hands. "There's something in my head! Get it out!" He collapsed on the floor, curling up in the fetal position, screaming incoherently.

The others weren't in better shape. One of them bent at the waist, arms over his torso, and retched into a bucket between his feet. Micah winced at what looked like blood pouring from the shifter's mouth. Another stood facing a corner, banging his head against the wall while two others tried to stop him. A third babbled incoherently, slamming his fists against a wooden table until it cracked in two.

There were six in all, Derek included, their cries filling the room along with panicked questions from those trying to settle them down. Micah's skin crawled at the sight and sound of it. He had once watched a documentary featuring an old asylum where the patients were left to suffer, and this wasn't too far from what he'd seen. Only that had been decades in the past.

"What did they take?" He asked the question of no one in particular and didn't expect an answer.

"Nothing." Jordan had bent over his son but somehow heard Micah's question over the screaming. He unfolded his large body, growling softly as he took in the sight of the three newcomers. "Do you think I would've called you here if my son and his friends were experimenting with drugs? This has been going on since last night, when they tried to shift before the hunt."

"They weren't able to shift?" Ezra exchanged a look with Micah, who understood why. It hadn't been more than two full moons that Ezra was able to shift and hunt with the pack again. He would take this harder than anyone else after suffering the sense of separation from his wolf.

Jordan shook his head, looking down at his son. "No. They were fine before they attempted it. Normal. They were out earlier in the evening, in town, but met up with us at the appointed time. I couldn't have guessed—" His voice broke. For the first time, it occurred to Micah that the alpha might actually love his son. That he saw him as more than his legacy.

All it took was agonized, ear-splitting screams to stir up that fatherly affection.

Ezra looked at Micah again, then at Adam. "It might not be my place to say this, but I went through something similar months ago."

"You went through this?" The hope in Jordan's voice was audible even with so much chaos around them. He went to Ezra, taking him by the shoulders. "What happened? How did you recover?"

Now it looked like he wished he'd never opened his mouth. "It was a witch. A curse. It separated me from my wolf. I was unable to shift or even feel the wolf inside me. It lasted months."

Jordan's jaw tightened, his teeth bared in a snarl. "Of course it was witchcraft. I should've guessed. I had my suspicions, in fact, but I didn't want to pin this on one thing or another before I learned everything possible."

As much as Micah hated to feed Jordan's legendary hatred of witches, there was no other explanation that made sense. Not that he could come up with, anyway. Shifters were the most powerful supernaturals in existence, at least as far as any of them knew. Possessed of great magic passed down through dozens of generations. Two beings in one, animal and human. It took an equally strong power to interfere with them.

Who else but a witch could be capable of this?

That didn't explain anything, though, did it? "Why would a witch do this? Has there been trouble with them?"

Jordan scowled at Micah's question. "When hasn't there been trouble with them? My father and grandfather were right. The entire race needs to be wiped from the planet. They bring nothing but—"

Adam cut him off. "I've heard rumors of attacks on witches. Attacks coming from shifters." When Jordan's expression went stony, Adam folded his arms and looked the other alpha up and down. "Wolves, in particular. Does that ring any bells?"

"What are you suggesting? That this is some sort of retaliation for whatever's going on—if anything's going on in the first place?" Jordan was no fool. He knew he needed to be careful with his language. Not that it mattered. He might as well have been made of glass, he was so transparent. "Besides, if it is, who's to say this won't affect another pack? Such as yours, for instance?"

Another careful choice of language. Adam couldn't dismiss the question, or else it would sound like he didn't care about the safety of the pack.

Jordan continued, his face slowly turning redder. "Besides, you've already described an attack on one of your members. Who's to say it can't happen again? Who's to say we aren't all in danger?" As if on cue, Derek unleashed another scream that sounded like it came from the depths of his soul.

Someone new entered the room, someone who tore through like a tornado before stopping beside

Derek and kneeling next to him. Micah fell back a step at her scent, one he hadn't picked up in ages.

"Derek? What's wrong, what happened?" She ran a hand over his head, gasping and flinching away when he howled in pain at her touch.

Marsha. Was there something between them? Micah hadn't so much as heard her name since the break-up. Interpack mingling was rare, especially when Jordan's pack was notoriously hot-headed and unpredictable, but he'd convinced himself Marsha was different. Maybe she was, too. That didn't mean they were meant for each other.

She tossed back her sandy curls before looking around the room in horror, her head swinging in all directions as she took in the sight of so much torment. "What's happening? Why?"

It seemed like he was the only one who heard her, the only one paying attention. He came closer, wanting to reach for her, knowing it would be a mistake. "That's what we're trying to find out."

She looked up at him, and at first, he was sure she didn't recognize him. Too panicked, too scared. She blinked, eyes filled with tears that made them look bluer than ever. "Micah? What are you doing here?"

He was about to answer when the shifter in the

corner collapsed, blood running down his face. He'd hit his head one too many times. Several of the unafflicted ran to him, pulled him into the center of the room, where he writhed and pled for help.

There was no telling if he'd heal quickly or not. No way of knowing how far this curse went, if it was a curse at all. Too many questions. Not enough answers.

And Marsha, kneeling next to Derek, trying in vain to comfort him. She reached down, trying to touch his shoulder, and he screamed like her hand was made of fire. "Get away from me!" It was a shriek, almost animal. "Don't touch me!" She recoiled before covering her face with her hands. The shaking of her shoulders told Micah she was weeping.

In the middle of all this, it seemed ridiculous to want to comfort her. She should've been the last thing on his mind, especially when their breakup hadn't been exactly friendly. Then she had always done a number on him, hadn't she?

He went to Ezra, leaning in to make sure his best friend heard him. "I need to get out of here."

Ezra needed no explanation. He was well aware of their history. "Go ahead. I'll keep you posted."

It was a relief to be out of there, even though the

screaming still echoed in Micah's head. He doubted he'd be able to forget it anytime soon. There was no love lost between him or any of the shifters going through torture, but he wouldn't wish that sort of agony on anybody.

How long could something like that go on before it killed them?

It took a few deep breaths once he was outside, standing in the courtyard of the enormous complex, to clear his head. The pair of guards at the gatehouse kept an eye on him—he could feel their stares, probably wondering what he was doing there. What would it be like, living that way? Always paranoid, watching for threats that might not exist.

Adam was a strong leader, the sort others couldn't help but follow. He didn't need to rule the pack using force or coercion. There was no paranoia, no need to use shadowy, theoretical threats to keep the members close. To keep them obedient.

A howl pierced the air, coming from inside the mansion. Not the howl of a wolf but rather of a shifter who'd made the mistake of trying to shift while under a witch's curse. So maybe there were threats out there, after all.

Part of him wondered if the pack didn't deserve this, at least somewhat. Jordan and those who came before him were never good to witches. Micah didn't exactly love them, but there was no reason to target them. For years there'd been rumors of pack members harassing witches on the streets of Shotgun Falls and larger towns and cities—even in Denver. Especially somewhere like Denver, crowded and busy. Less chance of retaliation out in the open.

Cowards, all of them. Bullies.

But Jordan had a point. If it could happen to their pack, it could happen anywhere. It was better to be on the lookout for trouble rather than assuming they were immune.

"THEY'RE STILL SUFFERING, but the physical effects seem to have calmed down a little. No more puking up blood or anything." Ezra paused. "But their mental state isn't any better. It might even be getting worse. They're raving, coming up with all kinds of crazy ideas. One of them started seeing things. Jordan had them all sedated."

It must've taken a heavy dose of whatever they used to put down six wolf shifters. "I've never heard anything like this before."

"None of us has. Whoever did this, they meant business."

Micah couldn't bring himself to feel smug or relieved it wasn't their pack under attack. A full day's sleep and hours spent mulling things over during the night hadn't eased the memory of those screams. Rather than try to forget about it, he decided to go out and do something. Whether or not it would be helpful was another story.

It was no secret where the Cedar Woods pack hunted. Their territory bordered the Shotgun Falls territory, as if the area had been split clean in half. He decided to head that way, to sniff things out. According to Ezra, Derek and the others had hunted there the two nights before the trouble started. It was as good a place to investigate as any.

He drove out to the border and stepped out of his truck. The sun was starting to set, and the temperature was beginning to drop. It would snow soon, the first of the season. Not that cold bothered him any. His wolf kept him warm, even while he was human.

Once he shifted, looking at the woods through his wolf's eyes, there was no missing what he'd been unable to sense as a man. It was one thing for another shifter to pass nearby—he could scent that at a thousand paces—but another to pick up the scent of a witch.

Now? It was clear as day. A witch had been nearby. Maybe more than one.

And they'd bled. He was no further than half a mile from the truck when he picked up the metallic aroma hanging in the air. He might not have caught it if rain or snow had fallen, but they'd enjoyed a string of dry days lately. There was nothing to wash it away.

His wolf growled, ears tuned to any unusual sounds. There was no one nearby. No cries or whimpers. The blood wasn't fresh. He decided to follow the trail, to see where it led while the sun sank behind the mountains.

"From what I hear, they're suffering terribly." Sylvia Redferne shook her head, making her silver braid swing from side to side. "I've never been a particular fan of that pack—sorry, I know you were once involved with the alpha's son —but I hate to hear of this kind of thing. I wouldn't wish it on anyone."

Esme made a sympathetic sound but didn't go so far as to agree with her cousin. If Sylvia hadn't been stripped of her powers years ago, she might've been able to sense what Esme had done. Now, there were still scraps of magic clinging to her like loose threads, but she might as well have been human for all the good they did.

"And how are you? I don't see you nearly

enough." Sylvia slid Esme's latest purchase into a paper bag before handing it over. Her bookstore was one of Esme's favorite places in all of Shotgun Falls. Maybe in the entire state. Not only was it chock full of rare and antique finds, but it was cozy. Welcoming. And Sylvia always offered a free cup of Esme's favorite tea.

"You know how it is. I keep to myself." Esme offered what she hoped was a convincing smile, full of confidence and bravery.

If her cousin knew better, she was kind enough to pretend otherwise. "Everything's well, though?"

"Better than well." Much better. Her smile widened, becoming more genuine. Was it wrong to feel a little proud, a little full of herself over what she'd managed to do? Knowing Derek and the rest of his buddies were suffering for their crimes was better than just about anything she could've hoped for. Sylvia wasn't the only one in town talking about it, either. Word had spread like wildfire.

Good. Let everybody know what happens when you torture innocent, helpless women.

"I'm happy to hear it. Speaking of happiness, Hope and the rest of her girlfriends were in here a few days back. You know how they like to get together here." Sylvia grinned. "They keep me young. Anyway, she made especially sure to remind me to say hello the next time I saw you. So, hello."

Hope was a nice person. Somebody Esme had been happy to help after Sylvia had practically banged down the cabin door, talking about big trouble. Another witch, a dark witch with a grudge, had cursed the shifter destined to be her mate. It had taken time to free Ezra of the curse, but it seemed like Esme's work had paid off. "I'm glad everything's okay with them."

Something passed over Sylvia's face, and Esme knew what she was about to say before she uttered the first word. "You know, the girls come in once a month or so. Perhaps you could join them next time. They're such a nice bunch."

"I'm sure they are, but—"

Sylvia's face fell. "I know. You can't hide forever, dear."

Frustration threatened to steal Esme's voice. That and the irritation she always experienced after being misunderstood. "I'm not hiding. I prefer living the way I do. And I'm never lonely." She lifted the bag holding her new book, one devoted to rare plants and herbal remedies.

"A house full of plants is no substitute for connection."

"I'm sure you're right." There was no taking about it, especially not here. There were customers everywhere, though it seemed most of them were more interested in the stories about the afflicted shifters than in rare books. Still, Sylvia had things to do, and Esme was in no mood to rehash what they'd already been through so many times.

She retreated to the beverage station, where one of Sylvia's employees fixed all kinds of sweet-smelling concoctions. "Esme. Your usual?"

The fact that she had a usual struck Esme as funny. She hardly ever ventured from the cabin except for her twice-monthly supply trips. "That would be great, thanks. It's cold out there."

"I'm sure you could use some tea to warm you up, then." Esme stepped aside for the next customer to place their order, looking around while she waited. A group of she-wolves sat in a cluster, perched on purple velvet chairs arranged around a marble-topped table. No one needed to announce who they were. Esme could feel the difference in their energy. It brought to mind her time with Ezra and that friend of his. Micah. Mr. Personality himself.

The concern etched on the faces of the women held her attention. Was she staring? None of them noticed. They were too deeply involved in their conversation, so much so that the air around them appeared to vibrate from the intensity. At least through Esme's eyes.

"I even warned Hope about it." One of them leaned closer, though she didn't lower her voice. Esme could hear her loud and clear. "I don't want him hunting without the pack. I don't want him out alone if possible."

Hope. Could it be? In fact, the woman looked a lot like Ezra. Softer, feminine, her dark hair touched with silver, but otherwise, they could be twins.

"What could she do about it?" Another of the women laughed, though there was no humor in it. "How many years have we wasted trying to tell our sons what to do? If they wouldn't listen to us, why would they listen to their mates?"

The first woman snickered. "Come on, now. We're all grown. We know the difference between a request from a parent and one from a mate."

Yes. They were talking about people Esme knew. She also knew Ezra wasn't part of Jordan's pack, but rather a member of the Shotgun Falls pack. She had no problems with them. She even liked them, if grudgingly. For the most part.

There was no way of sharing that. No way of

easing the mothers' minds. It would mean admitting she was behind the curse—while she wasn't the least bit sorry for what she'd done, she doubted a shifter would be forgiving, even one outside Derek's pack. There were fellow witches who'd feel the same.

But then they wouldn't understand, would they? Not unless they'd seen what she had.

It was time to go. She'd already spent too much time in town, anyway. The layers of protection she always wrapped around herself before heading out took a lot of energy to maintain, and the effort was starting to tire her out. The spell was weakening, too —the worry and helplessness of the mothers sitting nearby were starting to leak into Esme's energy field. Good thing the tea was ready. If she left without it, Sylvia would take it as a bad sign. As it was, her cousin was too busy with customers to notice her walking through the door and onto the sidewalk. It was for the best.

The air was bitingly cold. Esme blew out a long breath which hung in a cloud around her head. As important as spring and summer were, these colder, darker months were just as vital. The earth could rest, could replenish itself before bursting with new life. She always welcomed it, even looked forward to it. More reason to hole up in the cabin.

The groceries and other things she'd already picked up were in the trunk of her car, parked a block down from Sylvia's. She wasted no time getting there, more than ready to be home again. Alone. Why did the world always seem so much bigger with every visit she made? It was her brain playing tricks on her, of course. That and memory. Ugly, painful memory.

By the time she was behind the wheel with her tea in the cupholder, she'd almost forgotten all about how proud she'd been of herself earlier. Now she was too busy being grateful for the silence and stillness inside the car. The silence wasn't long-lasting, though, not once she turned the key and the radio came to life. She turned it to an oldies station and sang along, even though she knew she wasn't much of a singer. Another good thing about living alone: she could sing all day long, and there was nobody around to remind her how bad she sounded.

The sun had set by the time she made it home, her headlights sweeping over the familiar trees surrounding the cabin. They formed a perfect circle, those trees, sitting close enough together that they concealed the cabin from the average hiker. Not that she ran into many of them up here. The benefit of knowing how to whip up a spell to deter strangers.

They didn't know they were under the power of a witch, naturally. They only knew her particular part of the woods wasn't where they wanted to hike. They thought they were the ones making the decision for themselves, the way humans always did.

It was better that way. Fewer humans, fewer strangers. If a human ran into what looked to them like a girl in her early twenties living off the grid, virtually in the middle of nowhere, they'd make a big deal out of it. Probably put her up on social media, the way Sylvia and those pack mothers had forced the shifters to test a stupid dating app. Why they'd want to mix with the human world was a mystery, though it had seemed to work out for at least a couple of them. Ezra had found Hope. Logan Fournier had mated with another human girl. Charlotte, her name was. She seemed decent, too. Maybe it took a special kind of human to—

The front door was partly open.

Everything on Esme's mind blew apart and drifted away like smoke. She never left the door open, not even when she was going no further than to the garden under the kitchen window.

There was a shifter nearby, too. She smelled it, the scent wafting her way from inside her home. Her home! They had violated her by breaking into her home. The air around her crackled as anger rushed to the surface of her energy field. Whoever they were, she'd show them what happened to a shifter or to anybody who trespassed on her property.

Instead of emptying the trunk, she marched across the clearing and kicked the door open the rest of the way. With all the force in her, she bellowed into the dark cabin. "What do you think you're doing here?"

All she found was a shifter in front of her open refrigerator, one who pulled a bottle of water from the door before closing it. "Perfect timing." He popped open the cap before lowering himself into one of the chairs at the table, making himself comfortable.

That was when recognition passed between them. She knew he remembered her when his eyebrows shot up, practically leaving his forehead. "Oh. It's you."

Of all the shifters, she would've been content never to see again.

"Micah? What are you doing here?"

"Well?" She put her hands on her hips, tapping her foot against the wood floor. "I'm waiting for an explanation. What are you doing here?"

"I was going to ask you the same thing. Is this where you live?" He sucked down half the bottle of water before looking around himself. "I mean, it's nice enough, but this far away from town?"

"It's none of your business. And you still haven't told me what you're doing here."

"It's cold out there." He jerked his chin toward the open door. "Wanna close that?"

"You're the one who left it open after breaking in."

"I didn't break in. The door was unlocked. I only opened it."

"Wow." She shook her head slowly. "To think, I forgot why I don't like you. Thanks for reminding me."

Micah lifted his broad shoulders. "No problem." He peered past her, out the door. "You need help carrying anything inside?"

What was going on here? There was no making sense of it. Like she'd walked into a play halfway through the first act. Only she was one of the actors and hadn't so much as glanced at the script.

"I need help understanding what you're doing in my house, Micah."

"I'll tell you all about it, Esme." She didn't like the way his lips twitched when he said her name. Like this was all a game. "I'm trying to offer my assistance before we get down to business, because once we start talking about what led me here, I might not be in such a helpful mood anymore."

"I don't need your help." What was that fluttery feeling low in her belly? Not apprehension, surely. Definitely not fear. What did she have to be afraid of? This smirking, sarcastic jokester was the least of her problems. Even if he looked at her like they had a problem only he knew about—but was too eager to let her in on.

It was cold enough out there to keep her perishables safe. She wasn't about to turn her back on Micah. Who knew what he'd do?

"Fair enough. Can't say I didn't offer." He drained what was left in the bottle before crushing it in one hand. Not exactly impressive, though she had the feeling the gesture was intended with that in mind. "Do you want to tell me how I was able to follow a trail of blood to your front door, then? Would you rather discuss that?"

All of a sudden, the thought of getting groceries from the car was preferable.

Remember who you are. Right, and what was she thinking? She was no mere human girl. He might've been powerful, but she had powers of her own. Granted, her energy was low after spending hours in town, but she could still hold her own if he decided to attack.

Somehow she doubted that was what he had in mind. He didn't seem angry. Troubled, yes, but not angry. There was none of that dark, nasty energy rolling off him.

"Blood happens." She lifted a shoulder, enjoying

the way he rolled his eyes. "What do you want me to say?"

"I want you to tell me who was bleeding and how they made it all the way from Cedar Woods territory to your front door."

"That far?" It slipped out before she could stop herself.

His eyes lit up. "So you do know what I'm talking about?"

"No. Only that we're a couple of miles from the border."

His brows drew together like he was frustrated with her quick response. "Right. I'm sure."

"I don't know what you want me to say."

"I want you to tell me why a witch—and don't tell me it wasn't, I could smell the difference in the blood—came all that way and ended up here. At your cabin. Not long ago, either. I'd say within the last forty-eight hours. What was the problem?"

"What business is that of yours? Do I show up at your house and ask why it reeks of dog?"

"Watch it." There was an edge to his voice now. No more kidding around.

She refused to apologize, thought. "Wolf. Why it reeks of wolf."

When he stood, unfolding his enormous body,

her breath caught. It was easy to forget how big, how strong he was when they were sniping back and forth. Like they had at Ezra's. Now, with his fists clenched and his entire body vibrating with tension, she found it hard to catch her breath. Her heart pounded. What was this effect he had on her?

"Let's cut to the chase." He took one menacing step her way, then another. "What happened to the Cedar Woods pack? Who cursed them? Why did they do it?"

"Why are you asking me?"

His head tipped to the side, eyes flashing. Eyes that were beginning to swirl with a different sort of light. Amber light. His wolf was dangerously close to the surface. "You don't sound surprised."

"It was all I heard about in town. I stopped at Sylvia's."

"Oh. I see." He didn't seem satisfied, though. "So that was the first time you heard about it? You have no idea why a witch like yourself would want to cast a curse on the pack? So soon after a witch bled her way through the woods and landed on your doorstep? You realize I can still smell the blood in here. There was a lot of it."

His eyes flicked back and forth around him. "You

did a good job cleaning it up, but certain scents linger."

"Thank you?"

He snickered, easing a little of the tension, but not enough. "Tell me. Did she do it, whoever she is?"

"Why are you so determined to find out?"

Another step. He was coming too close. She backed away as casually as possible until she hit the wall behind her. "If it could happen to them, it could happen to us. Are you honestly pretending not to understand how this would affect other shifters?"

"I'm sure you'll be fine."

He came to a stop. "And how would you sound so sure if you didn't know who cast the curse? It was either you or the witch who came here. Who was it? Why was it cast?"

"It's none of your business."

"What a stupid thing to say. It might not be my pack going through hell right now, but it's my business. Unless and until I know why the curse exists, I can't believe it has nothing to do with me or my pack." His expression softened a little. "And I've seen what they're going through. With my own eyes. We're not friends, and I doubt we ever will be, but it was terrible."

"What a shame."

"So it was you." His eyes swirled again, reminding her who she was dealing with. "Only the witch who did this would be so flippant about it. What? Did you get bored and decide to drive a handful of shifters out of their minds?"

"Sure. I had nothing better to do." When he didn't back down, her anger grew. The light over the sink flickered. "You'd better get going. I've already extended more courtesy than I would to anyone else who entered my home without permission."

"What are you going to do? Call the police?"

"That's a funny question considering you just accused me of casting a curse that's driving shifters like yourself out of their minds. Why would I need to call the police?"

His energy thickened. Darkened. She felt his anger, but there was more to it than that. Irritation. Aggravation. He was at a loss, worried and confused. Maybe afraid for his friends, his pack.

There was something else, too. Something sharp. Bitter. Jealousy? Why would he feel that? He couldn't be jealous of Derek and his friends, for sure. Nobody would want to be in their shoes.

Before he could come up with something sarcastic to say, she lifted her chin. The height difference between them was sobering, even worrisome, but all she had to do was remind herself who she was. What she was capable of. She might as well be twice his height rather than what felt like half of it when he towered over her. "Get out of my way, then get out of my house. I don't want you here." When he didn't budge or even blink, staring at her with the same intensity, she narrowed her eyes. "Unless you'd like me to make it so you wish you had."

"Admit what you did to them."

"You aren't in any position to tell me what to do."

"I'm not? Then why are you trembling?"

"I'm not trembling."

"Liar. I can smell your fear. Or have you forgotten what shifters are capable of? You're not the only one with an edge here." Then, so softly she could barely hear it, he growled.

Point taken.

"Fine. You want to know? Yes. I cast the curse."

"Why would you do that?"

"Because of the witch whose blood you smelled. My friend." Her voice shook, but she didn't care enough to try to conceal it. Let him hear how upset she was, how angry and horrified for her friend. For herself. "She was one of four witches drugged down at the Full Moon bar, then brought to the woods. In Cedar Woods territory, by the way. Far from town but close enough to me that Amy was able to find her way, even as badly wounded as she was."

"What does that have to do with the pack?"

"Oh, come on." She tossed her head. "Don't act like you don't know. Everybody's heard about the things they do."

The one thing he wasn't experiencing was confusion. She felt his anger. His outrage at what she'd done. There was no confusion, though. "You already knew about it. Didn't you?"

He frowned, his forehead creasing. "Not really. People talk, but—"

"You knew. And you did nothing about it. This isn't the first time he's pulled something like what I described, either. Would you like to hear about how he and his friends chased Amy and the others through the woods? They were terrified. Still woozy from the drugs. Unable to use their powers thanks to some bracelets the pack put on them. Defenseless."

She gritted her teeth, determined to get through the rest without breaking down. "She was covered in bruises. Bites. Cuts, claw marks. They beat those girls within an inch of their lives and left them in a dried-up creek. And it wasn't the first time. You know it. I know it. And all you care about is what happens to the shifters. The poor, poor things."

For a long minute, all they did was glare at each other. His chest heaved, his nostrils flared, and a low growl rolled through him. Let him defend Derek. Let him say it meant nothing. She almost hoped he would, since that would give her more than enough reason to destroy him. Or at least to make him wish he'd responded otherwise.

Instead, he blew out a sharp breath. "Lift the curse."

"Make me."

A surprised laugh blurted out of him. "Really? That's what this is going to turn into? A childish fight?" All she did was shrug. "You don't care that this curse is going to start trouble between the shifters and witches in Shotgun Falls? Because it is. Pretty soon, things are going to start falling apart. They were strained enough before this."

He had a point. "I'm sure the fact that shifters are able to get away with torturing witches has nothing to do with it."

"Do me a favor and take that up with somebody who can do something about it."

"You're right." She smiled. "I doubt you have any sort of clout. Nobody would listen to you if you asked them to stop hunting witches instead of stag."

He growled louder than ever, telling her she was pushing too hard. "Listen. I can't lift the curse."

"Please."

"I mean it. Derek has to be the one to remove it."

He snickered, skeptical. Not that she could blame him, being a clueless shifter and everything. He might've had brawn on his side, but he knew nothing of real magic. "How would he do that?"

"By owning up to what he's done. No matter how terrible it is. He has to admit his crimes and accept responsibility." She rolled her eyes. "Not that he will. Owning up to his mistakes isn't something he was ever good at. Not that he tried."

His energy heightened, the heat from his body enough to make her perspire. "You don't know the sort of trouble you've put yourself in. I know you think you're doing what you have to do, but I'm not the only shifter who'll show up at your door if you don't do something about the curse. What will it take for you to understand that?" Was there a note of desperation in his words? She thought she heard it, felt it, but his anger was thicker. Stronger. Like storm clouds in front of the sun.

"I've already told you. There's nothing I can do about it."

He exhaled. "Then there's nothing I can do to help you."

"I'm surprised you'd want to help me at all." She looked him up and down, genuinely interested in his motives. "Why aren't you threatening to turn me in? I've admitted to putting members of your species through agonizing pain. You'd be a hero for taking me to Jordan and letting him deal with me. Why don't you?"

Not that she had any intention of letting him do that. More than that, she didn't believe he'd do it even if he made the threat. He didn't have the same nastiness Derek did. The same hardness. He wasn't as jaded—at least, he didn't strike her that way.

Instead of answering her question, Micah backed away, his hands still in fists at his sides. He snarled at her, baring his teeth. Then he stormed out, swinging the door hard enough that it crashed against the wall and bounced back, closing with a sharp click.

Only then could she relax, slumping against the wall.

If he'd found her and figured out what she did... who else might?

5

There was no shaking the idea that he'd made the biggest mistake in all his life.

It was better this way, wasn't it? Leaving her at the cabin, pretending he'd never been there. Not breathing a word of that visit to anybody in the pack. Not even Ezra.

No. Especially not Ezra. She held a special place in his heart—and in Hope's. If it hadn't been for her getting to the root of the curse Ezra had suffered from, he might still be without his wolf. Feeling like an outsider, ready to banish himself from the pack.

When Micah thought about it that way, he couldn't bring himself to be angry with the witch. Not angry enough to turn her over to Jordan. If Ezra found out, he'd be even more conflicted than Micah currently was.

There was something about her that got under his skin. It was the same way back at Ezra's. Though there had been others there, plenty of them, she had seemed to focus on him. Like his very existence bothered her. Worse than that, he'd felt the same. It had almost been fun to rattle her cage.

The same had been true at the cabin. He should've been ashamed of himself, firing off sarcastic comments, loving it when she'd fire one back. She deserved to be dragged out of that cabin by that red hair of hers. All the way through the woods, all the way back to Jordan's compound. Let them deal with her. Let them give her what she deserved.

This would've been a lot easier if he genuinely believed she deserved what Jordan would dole out.

And if he was in any position to condemn a witch for anything...

A burst of laughter from the other end of the room caught his attention. What was he doing here? When was the last time he'd visited the Full Moon? Once Esme had mentioned the name, it was all he could think of. Instead of driving home after reaching the truck, he'd come here.

Was it true? Derek and his friends were drugging witches? Rumors were one thing, but now he had mental images to pair up with those rumors. Witches running through the dark. Powerless. Frantic. Drugged.

And the howling and laughter behind them. The terror they must've gone through.

Did it soften the memory of watching Derek writhe and scream, though? What about the one in the corner, bashing his head against the walls until he bled? Esme was interfering with the fundamental nature of a supernatural, something witches were forbidden to do.

She had to know how dangerous this was. He stared down at his half-empty beer bottle, turning it in slow circles. The idea of the danger she was putting herself in made the wolf growl in his head, the sound louder than the game playing on the TV above the bar. Even shifters liked football.

If she knew the consequences, why did she do it? This wasn't some young, arrogant, clueless witch. A witch like that couldn't have reunited Ezra and his wolf.

Though she was still arrogant. Almost enough to make him like her.

Which was why he had a hard time believing

this was only about her friends. Sure, it was natural to be outraged when a friend was hurt the way Esme had described. He would've been ready to kill the ones who'd done it.

Would he take his life in his hands? Risk a war between shifters and witches? The situation between them was tenuous on a good day thanks to Jordan's attitude—and his complete inability to keep his thoughts to himself. All that business about wiping them from the face of the planet. Talk about archaic, not to mention sick.

It was tough to imagine Esme having not considered any of this. Which was why he found it equally tough to imagine her cursing Derek without having another reason. A more personal reason.

What if—

The door opened behind him, though that wasn't what made Micah look over his shoulder. It was the burst of voices that came with it.

He recognized them right away. They were at Jordan's mansion, part of his pack. The shifters who were trying to help the others afflicted by the curse. Eight of them in all. If they noticed Micah sitting alone, they didn't show it. He thought it was just as well. They weren't friends, no matter what was going on.

His heart sank when he noticed Marsha wasn't with them. What a laugh. What would he say to her even if she did show up? How are you? What's new? Are you dating that nasty alpha's son who you used to swear disgusted you? What changed your mind about him?

Yes, that would get him far. He wouldn't end up getting laughed out of the bar or anything like that. Amazing, really, the things a heart chose to hang on to. The resentment and jealousy that could still exist long after a man thought he'd ridded himself of it. And all it took was a glance, a single glimpse to bring everything back.

One thing was for sure: they looked like they'd been through twelve rounds, every one of them. There was no laughter, no joking. They weren't out to have a little fun and maybe get into trouble by the night's end. This was more a matter of needing to get away, out of the compound. Away from the screaming.

By then they'd be sedated, anyway, the way Ezra said. This was as good a time as any to get out and grab some fresh air and fresh ale. Micah nodded to one of them when their eyes met. After a moment's hesitation, the shifter nodded back.

He returned to his beer, which all of a sudden

didn't have much of a taste. Why had he come out anyway? Right. He wanted to get a feel for the Full Moon. The girl behind the bar—a shifter, like everybody else in the bar—placed a full bottle in front of him. When he lifted his brows, she shrugged. "You looked like you could use it."

Yeah, because I can't shake the feeling I'm betraying my pack and maybe my entire species by keeping quiet about the witch who cursed some of us. And that's not the half of it. He'd be lucky if that was only half the problem. "You must know how to spot a sad sack at a hundred paces after working here."

"Something like that." She glanced toward Jordan's pack members, clustered in a tight group around a pair of high-top tables near the back. "It doesn't take a psychic, you know?"

"Do you ever get witches in here?"

She hit him with a hard, suspicious look. Nobody had ever accused him of being good at subterfuge. "Sometimes. Why do you ask? Don't give me any of that anti-witch crap. You can leave if—"

"No, no." He held up his hands in a gesture of surrender, grinning. "That's not why I was asking."

She didn't look convinced. "Then why were you asking?"

He glanced toward the concerned pack members. They were busy being miserable. "I heard stories about witches getting drugged here. Dragged out to the woods, tortured."

The bartender grimaced—but she didn't shake her head or fake cluelessness. "I don't work every night. Let me say that right now. So I can't speak to the stuff that happens when I'm not here. But I try to keep an eye on things whenever I can, you know? Human guys do the same thing to human girls sometimes."

She was getting defensive. He could sense her walls going up. Soon, she wouldn't want to talk at all. "I know. Sometimes I feel like I should apologize just for being born male."

That got a grin out of her. Under other circumstances, this could've been a very different sort of conversation. She probably got a lot of that treatment, though. He wasn't keen on being just another one of the unoriginal guys hitting on her.

And he hated being unoriginal. Call him anything else, but never call him cliché.

"But yeah." She nodded slowly, disgust wrinkling her nose and narrowing her eyes. Some of the light left them, too. "No matter how we try to watch, there's just too much going on to keep tabs on everybody, all the time."

"Nobody's asking you to parent your patrons." He understood where she was coming from. He'd want to know he did his best to prevent the sort of thing Esme had described.

"Are you kidding?"

They both turned in the direction the sudden sharp, strained question had come from. One of the Cedar Woods pack had gotten a phone call. He looked around at his packmates, eyes wide. "They were sleeping. We left others to watch over the rooms." Was that fear in his voice? Micah thought so. He also thought this sounded very bad.

The shifter didn't see the sense in keeping his voice down, obviously. The moment he was off the phone, he made an announcement to his friends. "They got out. All of them. Jordan ordered a sweep of the grounds around the compound, but they haven't been located yet."

Micah's insides went cold. They were out. They were out of their minds, all of them, and out in the world. Where nobody could stop them.

Instinct tapped its way along the back of his mind, working its way to the forefront of his awareness. He'd always had stronger instincts than most of his kind. The ability to see through people, to read between the lines, to hear what wasn't spoken. Granted, he was the only one who knew why this was and intended to keep it that way for all his life, but it helped.

Just then, it helped him know exactly what Derek wanted. Exactly where he'd go.

And that was why he left a few bills on the bar without taking the time to count how much he was leaving. Why he took off at a near run and threw himself behind the wheel of his truck.

They were going after her. They had to be. Tires squealed as he peeled away from the curb and shot off into the night. *Let me be on time. Let me beat them there.* How long had they been missing before that phone call went through, though? He had no way of knowing. He could only floor the gas pedal and hope he'd make it before Derek did.

Her little Volvo was still parked outside, but that didn't mean anything. Her door was closed, too, but he couldn't let himself assume she was safe. He sniffed the air on stepping down from the cab and smelled the thing he'd dreaded throughout the drive.

Shifters. Several of them, their scent heavy in the air.

"Esme?" What was the point of trying to be quiet now? He knew what he'd find once he was inside the cabin.

There was no blood. He heaved a relieved sigh on seeing that much, but the rest didn't exactly comfort him: the overturned kitchen table and chairs, bits of broken dishes scattered all over the floor, the soup bubbling over on the stove. He turned off the flame. "Esme?" Not that it was any use. She wasn't here. He couldn't feel her presence.

But he could smell the shifters, along with another aroma. Tangy. Familiar.

There might not be blood in the cabin, but the scent hung in the air. Panic threatened to rise up and block out everything else. What would they do to her? And why did he care so much?

He closed his eyes, forcing himself to breathe slowly, to pick up Esme's scent. It wasn't difficult.

He opened the door, sniffing the air again, this time focused solely on Esme. The wind carried her to him, turning him toward the west. Toward Cedar Woods territory. That was where they were taking her.

He followed as the season's first snowflakes began to drift down.

6
———

It was so cold. Freezing. She shivered until her teeth chattered. Why had she gone out without a coat on? Even without the help of a forecast, it was obvious there'd be snow by the time morning came. She could smell it in the air. Why would she go out in nothing but a thin sweater and jeans?

Why had she gone out at all?

Where was she?

Esme's eyelids fluttered open. All she saw around her was darkness. Complete dark, the sort that only existed deep in the woods. And snow. There was a thin crust of it on the ground but more was falling, clinging to her hair and landing on her eyelashes. She tried to brush them away and realized her hands were bound together, the ends of the rope then tied to a low limb.

That was when it all came back.

The cabin. Fixing supper. She had just turned on the flame under a pot of vegetable soup when she'd sensed them. Felt them. The thick, roiling rage, enough to choke her.

It was too late by then. Derek, his friends, they were already at her door by the time she'd turned, ready to use her magic to stop them. The last clear image she held was of the door swinging open—slowly, much slower than she would've guessed. Like he was drawing it out. Playing with her.

He was still playing.

She was alone, at least by the looks of it. Not by the feel of it, though. She could feel them somewhere nearby. Their anger. Their glee. Their insanity, clinging to her like so many perfect little snowflakes.

The ropes chafed her wrists as she got on her feet, feeling a little woozy but no longer confused. She tried to free herself, but that only made it worse, made the rope bite into her skin. There was a soft laugh from somewhere in the trees when she sucked in a pained breath. Her heart pounded sickeningly hard and fast, cold sweat now dampening the back of her neck.

She called upon her magic, hoping to break down the rope's fibers until it weakened, but it wouldn't work no matter how hard she concentrated. For one brief, sickening moment, she thought her magic had left her because of the curse. Because she'd misused it, turning her powers toward vengeance. The goddess had punished her.

No, that wasn't the reason. There was more than rope around her wrists.

There was a bracelet, too. Her stomach clenched, and her heart threatened to pound its way out of her chest when she recognized it. Thick links, a metal she couldn't identify. It must be imbued with dark magic, though she couldn't imagine the source. Or just why a shifter would have access to anything cursed by a dark witch. She had never been able to come up with an explanation since the first time she'd encountered it.

It burned her wrist, whatever it was made of. Not enough to melt her skin or flesh, not even enough to leave blisters. Like holding her wrist high above the gas jets of her stove, lowering it until the discomfort was too much. Right on the line between discomfort and pain.

She winced again, and again the sound of laughter floated her way. She shivered more from apprehension than the cold, though the cold wasn't exactly helping. "Cowards. It isn't enough to outnumber a witch. You have to make sure she can't use her powers, too."

Snow crunched somewhere ahead of her. She braced herself, her breath coming in short gasps and her heart threatening to burst free of her chest. "You've been a bad girl, Esme."

To think, there was a time she loved hearing him say her name. "Derek. What do you think you're doing? Why are you—"

"Don't bother with the lies." He came into view, and she wished he hadn't. The look in his eyes was unlike anything she'd seen before. Only one word came to mind when she saw that bright light: Madness. "We both know what you did. I could still smell that witch's blood all around your house. One of them went to you afterward."

She lifted her chin, forcing herself to look him in the eye as he sauntered toward her, his friends now coming into view behind him. "Afterward? After what, Derek? What did you do?"

"Enough. You're stalling now." Meanwhile, the

others surrounded the tree. There were six of them in all, and they all wore the same crazed look.

It wasn't the look of them that made perspiration turn to full-on sweat. It was their breathing. The sound of it. Primal. Insane. They couldn't wait to tear into her, even without the benefit of shifting into their wolves. She tugged the ropes, and one of them laughed.

"So, what? This is how you expect to end this? By kidnapping me and tying me to a tree? Using one of these bracelets on me?" She paused when her throat tightened but fought it off. "Again? Because you didn't get rid of me the first time, did you? What, you want to finish the job this time?"

Stupid question. His mouth spread in a grotesque parody of a smile. "You always could read my mind, Esme."

"Which is how I knew you were the one who tortured those witches."

He scoffed. "Whatever. I don't think I have to explain how this is going to go, then, since you're so good at looking inside my mind." One of the other shifters snarled, snaping his jaws like he could hardly wait to take a bite of her, but Derek ignored it. "You're going to lift this curse, and you're going to lift it now."

"I can't."

"Liar."

"It's not a lie." She blinked away the snow falling in her eyes, raising an arm to wipe it away as best she could. "It's the truth. I can't lift the curse. You have to be the one to do it."

"More lies." He folded his thick arms, his smile widening. "Why would I know how to lift a curse? I'm not a filthy, lying witch."

"You don't have to know magic. You only have to—"

"Enough." His voice snapped her head back from its forcefulness, the rage beneath it. "Tonight, you're going to pay for what you've done. It didn't have to be this way. You only had to undo this."

"Derek." She hated the pleading tone in her voice, but there was no fighting it. "Don't. Just listen to me for once." It was too late for that. Getting him to listen to reason was difficult enough when he wasn't insane.

"I'll give you one more chance." He stepped back, signaling for one of his friends to untie her. "You're going to get a ten-second head start. After that, we're coming after you."

"No. Don't do this." When he only laughed,

something inside her snapped. "Haven't you done enough to me? Wasn't it enough last time?"

For a second, he almost looked sorry. "It would've been, but you obviously forget the lesson. Don't worry. I'll make sure you never forget again." They laughed, all of them, and the sound was like knives driving into Esme's ears.

It was no use, running. They would catch her even without the ability to shift. Their senses were sharper than humans, their eyesight stronger even when they walked on two legs. She had no idea where they'd brought her—their territory, no doubt, but it covered miles and miles. She might run for two or three miles before even finding a road.

And they'd be able to see her, anyway. It didn't matter how she ran or whether she was able to hide. They'd smell her even now. This would only delay the inevitable.

What was the alternative? Standing in front of the tree, waiting for them to tear her apart? She wouldn't make it that easy. She could at least make them work for it.

Which was why she broke into a run the second she was free. The rope hadn't hit the ground before she took off, her boots sliding on the slick, snow-covered ground. They gave her at least some traction, and she took advantage, throwing herself forward, moving blindly. Desperately.

And behind her, laughter. High-pitched, edged with madness. "One!" Derek's voice rose above all of it, even above the deafening roar of blood rushing in her ears. "Two!"

Even though she knew it was a game, that they'd catch her anyway, that they might not even wait until he got to ten, she raced against time. Against the count of ten. Eight counts to go. Her foot slipped, and she fell against a tree whose low branches tore at her sweater. She pushed away from it, stumbling forward.

"Three! You'd better move faster than this! We can still see you!" At that, the others laughed like a pack of hyenas. "Four!"

Go, go, run. But where? There was no escaping. It all looked the same in all directions. Darkness. Trees. Roots reaching up out of the ground and trip-ping her. She stumbled over one of them, landing on one knee. White-hot pain shot up through her leg— she bit down on her lip to stifle a scream, fumbling her way to her feet and forcing herself forward.

"Five!" He sounded closer than before. They were already following slowly, taking their time. Savoring her panic. "Six!"

Her head snapped back and forth. It was snowing harder, making it even more difficult to see past what was immediately in front of her. The idea of climbing a tree flashed through her mind, but what was the use of that? They'd climb up easily and might throw her down and break her neck.

That might be better than what they had planned.

"Hurry up, Esme! We're right behind you!" They were, too. She could hear them crashing through the brush, laughing and calling her name. "Seven!"

She slid a finger under the bracelet and tugged in a last-ditch effort to break the links. It only intensified the dull burning sensation. Every breath of cold air she sucked into her lungs burned like fire, too. But she couldn't stop. She wouldn't.

Until she did, her feet tangling up in a series of gnarled roots covered in snow. She fell forward, striking her knees, skinning her palms. This time there was no hope of biting back a cry of pain and surprise.

"Gotcha." How he'd caught her so easily still came as a shock, even when she knew he'd been right behind her all the time. Derek took her by the waist and lifted her like she was weightless, throwing her against the nearest tree and knocking the air from her lungs.

She opened her mouth, ready to beg—no matter how much she didn't want to give him the satisfaction—but he closed a hand around her throat before she had the chance to even whimper. He came in close, his breath hot on her face. "It's a shame you couldn't learn your lesson."

He then threw her to the ground, where she landed on her already smarting hands and knees. His friends gathered around them, panting now, practically slobbering. She only got a glimpse of their feet before being hauled to hers again by a pair of unseen hands.

Somebody slapped her, and she spun halfway around before another slap sent her in the other direction, pain exploding in her head. Something deep inside told her to fight, to not make this so easy, but it was no use. There were too many of them. They were too strong. She was defenseless and exhausted and so, so afraid.

He was going to kill her. She saw it in his eyes when they came face-to-face again. Purple streaked with silver, churning like storm clouds. "One less witch in the world." Those were the last words he muttered before something bit into her side. Something with fire in it.

She fell to her knees, pressing a hand to her side. Warm. Wet. Blood.

A roar ripped through the air. Animal. Fierce, snarling. Tawny fur. Her panicked brain couldn't keep up, but somehow, she knew she was better off now. Someone was here to fight for her.

And he did, whoever he was. They were no match for the massive wolf whose jaws snapped, saliva dripping from them. He growled long and low. Menacing. Forbidding.

She blinked, squinting up at them, the snow falling harder now. It was hard to see, but she thought she made out the shapes of Derek and his friends backing away, cursing and muttering threats but helpless against the wolf. A few of them disappeared entirely, but Derek stood his ground. "You're going to regret this." He didn't sound like himself anymore.

The wolf only let out a hair-raising growl, advancing on Derek until he had no choice but to back away, fading into the darkness. The wolf then turned, finding Esme on the ground. She barely had the strength to keep her eyes open—blood flowed from her side, more all the time.

"Don't hurt me." It was all she could manage, that pitiful, whispered plea. The wolf loomed over her, its breath a cloud around its head.

Until it shifted. Until tawny fur became blond hair, and a pair of somewhat familiar eyes met hers. "Micah?" It made no sense. She had to be dreaming. Just as she dreamed him lifting her from the blood-splattered snow, clutching her to his chest before sprinting deeper into the woods.

The last thing she heard was Derek's crazed screaming before darkness closed in.

7

Now he'd done it. Now he'd really gone and scored himself an enemy. More than one of them.

Where was it? The old cabin he'd passed on his way to finding Esme. The snow had a funny way of making things appear different than they did not long ago, when Micah had shot past it like a bullet from a gun. He'd only barely registered the structure's presence on the way past. Now, it seemed that was where he needed to go. He had to get her to shelter, had to take a look at the wound in her side.

The blood soaked into his shirt, warm and wet in contrast to the snow now falling at a fast clip. Not that snow mattered much to him—it melted on contact with his skin and clothes. He barely felt the difference in the temperature, his inner warmth providing all the comfort he needed. But that wouldn't be the same for her. And she was still losing blood.

He paused, looking down at the witch. She was unconscious, the way she'd been since not long after he'd made his escape. He heard her heart beating, a slow but steady rhythm. Not very strong, though. How strong could she be, as small as she was? How much blood could she stand to lose?

One thing was for sure: Derek and the others would be able to scent her blood, even with the snow falling like it was. It might take more time than if the weather was dry, but eventually, they would pick her up. They would follow Micah's progress into the woods. They wouldn't stop, either, he knew that much. He had never seen insanity like what he'd witnessed tonight.

He moved forward with new urgency, determined to find the cabin which really was no more than a shack. It had a roof, though, and would keep her dry. If need be, he would keep her warm, too. Though that would do nothing for her wounds.

Then he found it, the shape appearing after a few minutes more. There was no scent of human or animal anywhere nearby, telling him the place had been abandoned for some time now. He kicked open the door, which offered no resistance, before stepping inside. His heightened vision allowed him to look around, to get a sense of what waited in there.

In short, there wasn't much. An old cot, a thin mattress on top. It was stained, torn open in a few spots, but he decided it was better than a hard, splintered floor. Still, he held her with one arm while flipping the mattress with the other hand. It was better on that side.

He grimaced, realizing their clothes were stuck together thanks to her blood. It had already begun to dry. That meant her sweater would be stuck to her skin, to her wound. She wouldn't much like it when he tried to peel it away, but he'd have to get a look at what Derek had done. Granted, he wasn't exactly skilled in the art of healing injuries. Shifters didn't have to worry about that. How was he supposed to help her?

First things first. He lowered her to the mattress and left her as she was, looking around to find any tools or instruments that might've been left behind by the last hunters to use this cabin. They dotted the woods, the mountainside, though it was obvious this one had been abandoned for ages. They were still in Jordan's territory. He wondered if their pack was as tolerant of hunters as his. It was doubtful. They weren't very tolerant of humans on the whole, and hunters were sometimes seen as infringing on a pack's food. At least, that was the excuse some shifters used when really, they didn't want to deal with humans and needed a reason to run them off.

There was no running water, but there was a bucket near the door. How far to the nearest stream? That didn't matter, because he didn't want to leave her alone. He doubted she would die on him, but shifters would pick up her scent even when they were human. There was no telling how long it would take between picking up Derek's scent nearby and catching sight of him, catching up to him, and keeping him out of the cabin.

Bottom line: If Derek or the others were close enough for their scent to hang in the air, it would mean them being able to smell Esme's blood. They would waste no time once that happened.

So instead of going in search of water, Micah went outside and scooped fresh snow into the bucket. The next question: should he light a fire? It was a risk, but so was leaving Esme in the cold. Sure, there was a roof over her head now, but all that did was keep the snow from landing on her. If he was going to melt the snow and heat it, there would have to be a fire involved. At least the falling snow would keep the smoke under control... or so he hoped. The fact was, he was guessing, hoping. Searching blindly for the next thing to do.

The box of matches on the mantle above the hearth was a godsend. So were the few bits of wood stacked against the wall—old, but dry. He lit the old leaves which had drifted down from the chimney, and they caught easily. Soon the room was warmer, brighter. He left the bucket near enough to the fire that the snow began to melt.

If only he had some sort of a blanket to give her, but there was nothing like that here. Of course, she wasn't wearing a jacket. He doubted Derek gave her the chance to grab it before pulling her from her cabin. She must've been terrified. She certainly was when he found her, surrounded by bloodthirsty shifters. Anybody would be.

He settled for dragging the cot closer to the fire. Now, he could see her clearly, along with the wound to her side. The sweater was tattered on that side, stuck to her skin the way he knew it would be, but he could see the gash clearly enough. Not too deep, but long. It didn't look to be actively bleeding anymore. He took that as a good sign.

Once the snow had melted and wasn't so cold to

the touch, he rolled Esme onto her good side, leaving the wound facing up. "You're not going to like this." She couldn't hear him, and he hoped against hope that she would stay unconscious while he did this.

Her arm fell to the side, behind her, and for the first time, he noticed a bracelet around her wrist. She wasn't wearing it before, at her cabin—he would've noticed it, the wide links glinting in the firelight. Was this the bracelet she was talking about, the one the witches were wearing when Derek chased them through the woods?

They had taken away her powers. They had left her defenseless. His wolf growled, the sound reverberating in his head, his chest. Only then did he realize he was growling out loud.

When he touched the metal, it was warm. Warmer than it should've been, for sure. What sort of powers did have? It might've been too strong for a powerless witch to break, but not for a shifter. He managed to work a finger between the links and Esme's raw, chafed skin. A quick tug and the bracelet broke, dropping to the floor. "We'll see if that helps you any." She couldn't hear him. It was just as well.

He lifted the sweater, wincing as the stiffened fibers peeled away from her skin. Her heartbeat was a steady rhythm in his head, like music playing underneath the scene in a movie. It didn't quicken, and he took that as a good sign. She was too far away to feel any of this.

He would need a rag, something to wash her with. The only solution was his shirt, which he took off without hesitation before dipping a sleeve into the bucket. If only Ezra could see him now, playing nurse to a wounded witch without so much as a clean towel to dry her with.

He went as gently as he could, wiping away the dried blood, until finally, there was a clear view of the damage Derek had done. He was wrong about the bleeding having stopped, though now it wasn't much more than a slow oozing. He figured that was to be expected. It would eventually close over, wouldn't it? He didn't have the first idea. If he was the one who'd been slashed, the wound would already have healed.

At least she was clean now. The thought of covering her with that blood-soaked sweater didn't seem right, though. She wore a bra underneath, and a thin tank top over it. "You're going to hate me for this." Maybe he'd get lucky, and she'd stay unconscious until the sweater dried. He took it off her as gently as he could, then dumped it repeatedly into the bucket until most of the blood was washed away. He wrung it out, then hung it over the edge of the cot closest to the fire, where steam rose from it. He'd let her decide if she wanted to keep the tank. For now, he left it bunched up around her chest so he could keep an eye on her wound.

He emptied the bucket outside, kicking more snow over the ground where it landed in hopes of covering up the aroma of blood. Then he filled it with new snow and left it to melt again. She would need to drink when she woke up. He needed water, too, and a little food wouldn't hurt after so much exertion. Hunting was just as out of the question as searching for a stream, of course. It would have to wait until he got home.

Only when would that be? They couldn't wait too long, that much was for sure, but they were deep in Cedar Woods territory. It would take time to cross on foot with a wounded witch. Derek and his friends would be scouring the woods now, more determined than ever to get their hands on Esme. And on him, though he was nowhere near as concerned for himself. He had the advantage. They still couldn't shift.

But they'd want to hurt him. He was under no illusions.

Esme's whimpers brought him back to her side. Her forehead creased when she whimpered again, brows drawing together over a scrunched face. A nice face, one he found himself studying even after she calmed down. The one thing he could remember from their first interactions—besides how she got under his skin—was how beautiful she was. Small, delicate features to go along with a small, delicate body. Her bow-shaped upper lip quivered like she was ready to whimper again. When he brushed a hand over her short, vibrant hair, the quivering stopped. It would be stupid to think he was the reason she felt comforted, right? Then why couldn't he stop himself from thinking it?

On the whole, she wasn't bad-looking at all. For a witch, anyway. Not that he had any room to talk. He reached out again, prepared to stroke her soft, thick hair.

Her eyes flew open. Bright, too bright, filled with terror. "No. No!"

"Shh." He couldn't let her thrash around, and she was roughly two seconds from doing just that. "Shh, take it easy. You're safe. It's me. It's Micah." Her heart was beating too fast, the rhythm doubling and even tripling.

She blinked hard. He wondered if she heard

him. "You're safe now, but you have to stay still. You're wounded. You don't want to open it up again."

Finally, understanding touched her eyes. Loosened her muscles. She stopped fighting, stopped trying to get up. "Micah? Why? Why did you do that? Why did you come after me?"

What was he supposed to say? That he felt sorry for her, even if he knew she brought this on herself with that curse? That nobody deserved what Derek planned to do to her? That his sense of justice wouldn't let him sleep at night if he hadn't stepped in?

That they weren't as different as she thought they were?

He could've said any of it, but the connection between brain and mouth didn't seem to be working. Not with her glaring at him in confusion, in fear. Of course, she'd still be afraid. Anybody would be. He sensed that confusion, that helplessness, and it touched him.

To the point where there was nothing left for him to do but kiss her.

8

What the—?

One second she was fighting to make sense of everything that happened. Where she was, how she'd gotten there, how far she was from home. Why in the world Micah, of all people, had rescued her. And why she was in so much pain.

The next?

He was kissing her. As if his rescue wasn't confusing enough. Now she had to ask herself why he would do this. He hated her—they hadn't gotten along for one second since they met.

He wasn't a bad kisser, though. Slow, deliberate. Like he believed in taking his time to get it right.

And he was getting it right, for sure, undoing her with every brush of his strong, firm lips against hers.

It didn't last long. She wasn't sure whether that was a good or a bad thing. Her heart sank inexplicably when he ended it, almost jumping to his feet. He was shirtless, and the light from the fire played over his obscenely large muscles, his chiseled torso. "Sorry." She could barely make it out, a garbled grunt with his back turned. The way it moved, expanding and contracting almost wildly, told her he was breathing heavy. Hard. But why?

"I mean, you rescued me. I guess I owed you a kiss." She tried to laugh it off because, for some bizarre reason, it seemed like the right thing to do. To make him feel better, to soothe him when he was the one who'd gone ahead and kissed her without her consent. Why should she try to spare his feelings? "I wouldn't make a habit of it or anything, though. Don't go getting any ideas."

He snickered, his back still turned. "Only you would get sarcastic with me in this condition."

This condition. Right. The burning pain in her side. "Why am I half undressed?" She looked down at herself, her exposed skin, and that coupled with Micah's shirtless state only worsened what was already a confusing situation.

"Relax. Your sweater's hanging off the cot, drying." He turned his head partway, looking at her from the corner of his eye. "I figured you wouldn't appreciate it the way it was."

One look at the ruined garment confirmed what he was saying. He had tried to wash it, but there was only so much to be done for blood. It must've been gruesome before the washing. "Thank you. That was thoughtful."

"So I'm thoughtful now? Which is it?"

"Enough, okay?" As if her head wasn't jumbled up already. "I don't have it in me to bicker, as much as I enjoy it." The funniest thing of all: she wasn't lying. There was part of her, a large part, that enjoyed going toe to toe with him. It was rare to find someone willing to engage in wordplay. And she had been on her own for a long time. She was starved for conversation.

That had to be why he appealed to her the way he did. Not because she was attracted to him or anything like that. A sentient houseplant with a sense of humor would've been just as interesting.

She looked around, craning her neck to see in all directions. "How did you know about this place?"

"I passed it on the way to find you." He turned, folding his arms. The man was determined to tempt her, wasn't he? She concentrated on keeping her eyes away from his impressive biceps and shoulders, not to mention a set of pecs any bodybuilder would kill for. "You needed shelter more than anything else. And warmth."

She was warm, too. Almost cozy. How bizarre, feeling cozy and comfortable in a situation like this. An abandoned cabin decorated with webs and dust. Lying on an old cot that probably crawled with any number of bugs and mites. Micah's Henley draped over her.

Afraid of what it all meant.

Rather than giving in to that fear, she gritted her teeth against it. "Where are we, though? Your pack's territory?" She crossed her fingers and held her breath.

His shoulders fell an inch, and she released that breath. "Afraid not. I don't know exactly where we are—how far from the border, I mean. It took a lot of running to find you."

Every answer only inspired another question. They could spend all night like this, going back and forth. Something told her she wouldn't be any closer to understanding any of it by the time dawn came.

There was only one thing to say. "Thank you. I

don't know why you did it. Going to all that trouble, I mean. But I'm glad you did."

He hesitated—then smiled. A real smile, one that lit up his face. How unfortunate. He was even hotter this way. "Yeah, well, I didn't have anything better going on tonight."

She smiled, too, though briefly. There was too much pain in her side, not to mention her knees and hands and everywhere else. "I'm glad I got kidnapped on a slow night for you."

"Me, too. Sincerely." He came to her, crouching next to the cot. "When I heard they got loose, I knew he'd want to go for you."

"How did you know that?"

Why did he hesitate? There was a split second when she was sure he was about to say something important. He certainly looked like he was going to. But it passed before she was sure she wasn't imagining it. "Instinct. Besides, if I tracked the blood all the way to your house, I knew he would, too. He'd put it together—your friend going to your cabin after the attack."

"That makes sense. I'm glad you aren't as stupid as I assumed you were."

He winced. "Ouch." But there was a twinkle in

his eye. Were they honestly doing this? Joking? Even flirting, as disgusting as the idea was?

A memory crashed into her, making her forget everything in favor of looking at her wrist. A little chafed, a little red, but no bracelet now. "Where did it go? The bracelet?"

"I broke it." He reached down, and now she saw the pile of links on the floor. Before he could touch it she reached out and swatted his hand away.

"Don't touch it. We don't know where it came from or what makes it the way it is. You don't need to invite more trouble when you already got into enough tonight."

"Fair enough." He scowled, though, looking down at the broken bracelet. "Dark magic."

"I'm sure of it." She pushed herself up on her right arm, intending to sit up and test her strength, but searing pain in her side froze her in place. She sucked in a pained breath, even whimpering through clenched teeth before sinking back onto the cot.

"Take it easy. He got you good." No need to ask who Micah meant. "You don't want it to open up again. It bled pretty heavily for a while."

"No wonder I feel so weak." It wasn't an easy thing to admit, but what was the point of pretending? They were past that point. "What if the knife or whatever it was had magic, too?"

"What if it did? What could it do to you?"

"How much time do you have?" She tried to grin but suspected it looked more like a grimace. "I don't feel like it had magic. I would, too, if it did. The way the bracelet burned a little."

"I guess that's a good sign." He watched silently as she flexed her fingers in preparation of a healing spell. It would take all of her concentration when she was in this condition, but she'd have to manage it. Otherwise, she'd never be able to move from this spot.

Micah propped her up so she could hold both hands roughly an inch over the wound. She closed her eyes, summoning the goddess, never doubting her powers would serve.

Yet when her eyes opened, she found no change. No ball of light emanating from her palms. No sizzling sensation as her flesh began to mend itself. Nothing at all. "You have to be kidding."

"What's wrong?"

"You're asking the wrong person. I'm just as confused as you are." She took a deep breath and tried again, but this attempt was just as useless. A waste of time.

"What if the bracelet has a delayed reaction? You know? It might take a few hours for the dark magic to work its way out of your system."

She fought the impulse to laugh at what sounded like a child's hopeful wishes. He was doing his best, just like he'd done his best to take care of her. That alone was enough to earn her respect. "That could be. I guess it doesn't help us much right now, though, does it?"

He didn't match her attempt at being light-hearted. "No, it doesn't. Which is a shame since we need to get moving. Now, if possible."

"Right now?" The windows were filthy, but she could still see through them. Enough to make out the snow and the dark sky. "In the middle of the night?"

"Do you think Derek will wait until morning and resume the search?" He stood, grunting, muttering curses under his breath. "They escaped Jordan's compound, all of them. I'm sure Jordan has pack members searching the woods. There's nowhere for them to go, nowhere safe anyway. That's not what they're out for now. They're out to find you, and they'll either do that, or they'll be caught first."

"Then I guess we can only hope they're caught."

"Just the same, I'd rather not hang around in

hopes of that happening, you know?" He went to the window, peering out. She reminded herself he could see better in the dark than she could. "It can't be much past midnight, maybe one o'clock. I'd rather have darkness on my side if we're going to make the trek to my territory."

"And you don't know how far we are from that?"

"Not a clue. Not really. I only know it's going to take a lot of time to get there if I can't run." He looked over his shoulder. "I managed to move pretty fast when you were unconscious, but I jostled you around a lot. I don't think you'd like it much, and we can risk reopening the wound and having you bleed all over the place. They'd pick up the scent in no time."

Of course. He didn't care if she bled half to death, only that she not draw attention to them. It was stupid to even imagine for a second that he was going through this on her behalf. He probably wanted to avoid a war between the witches and the shifters and knew a dead witch would be all it took to spark a disaster. No way any of her kind would have to wonder for long who was responsible for her murder.

"So I guess I'm walking." She sat up, this time forcing herself to bear the pain, one hand pressed to her side. A little more blood oozed from the gash, but it didn't seem like an alarming amount.

"I wish there was something to bandage you with." Yes, he was reading her mind.

"I'll use this for now." She took the hem of her tank top in hand, then glanced up at him. "Would you mind...?"

Did he blush a little when he understood what she was about to do? She pressed her lips tight together to keep from giggling at his sudden embarrassment. He turned, and she did her best to peel off the tank without raising her left arm and aggravating the wound worse than ever.

Once it was off, she tied it around her midsection. It was impossible to cinch the two ends as tight as she'd need to, though, without the torn muscles in her side screaming in protest. There was no way around this. *At least I wore a pretty bra today.* "I need your help. I can't tie it off."

He turned slowly, jaw tight. That was all she managed to catch sight of before averting her eyes, embarrassment now turning her skin pink. Of all things to care about at a time like this. He could've stripped her naked when she was unconscious, and she wouldn't have the first idea.

Though in her heart, she doubted he would even

think about it. He might've been nothing but a shifter, and one who irritated the daylights out of her on top of that, but he wasn't the type to take advantage. That much she knew. That much she didn't need use of her powers to figure out.

Her powers. When would they come back?

She stiffened, grunting when he cinched the cotton tight enough to steal her breath. That was how it had to be, though. "Thanks." She reached for her sweater, and he handed it to her. It was dry already. "How isn't it even damp?"

"I squeezed as much of the water out as I could." That made sense. She would've struggled to do that with her bare hands, without magic, but it must've been easy for someone as strong as him.

"Thanks for that. Thanks for all of this." When he lifted a shoulder, it only annoyed her for some reason. Nobody wanted their thanks shrugged off. "I mean it. I know the sort of trouble you could've caused yourself by doing this, but you did it anyway. And you've taken good care of me. It means more than I can say."

And that little speech alone was enough to exhaust her. How was she supposed to make it home when she couldn't string a half-dozen sentences together without getting winded?

No time to worry about that now. He helped her into her sweater, then shrugged into his Henley. Her blood stained the front. She tried not to look at it, not to think about what it meant. What would've happened if he hadn't made it in time? What if he'd been just a few minutes later?

No time to worry about that, either. She could mull it over at home, where she'd be safe. It would take another few layers of protection spells to make that possible, though. Derek had certainly marched right in regardless of what she'd already put in place.

It could all be worked out later. For now, they had to move. No matter how much it hurt.

9

They were moving too slowly. *She* was moving too slowly.

"Let me carry you." He helped her over a fallen tree, painfully aware of the way she winced at the effort. He was doing all the work, and she was still in too much pain to hide it. But she was still too stubborn to accept anything more than support as they stumbled through the woods together.

"I told you. I don't need you to carry me." Her voice was sharp with irritation and pain. Probably more of the latter. This was absurd. Was he supposed to pretend she was in better shape than she was?

"We need to move faster than this. They've already had too much time to follow your scent."

"I thought you said the snow helped."

"It does help. Precipitation helps contain the scent and keeps it from spreading. But it doesn't wipe the scent out completely. If they happened to wander in the right—or wrong—direction..."

"I get it." But she wouldn't give in. Her stubbornness was going to get her killed.

He knew better than to say that out loud. It would be cruel, even if it was true.

They kept moving, then, making slow progress. At least the flakes were falling thick enough to cover the footprints they left. She shivered, her teeth chattering, and his heart went out to her for a second before he reminded himself she was the one to blame. For this, anyway. For refusing to admit she was in need of help.

They were heading west as far as Micah could tell. If it wasn't for the cloud cover, he'd know better, but then without the clouds, there would be no snow. No hope of concealing their progress.

She shook flakes from her hair before they could melt there. Soft hair. He remembered the feel of it, the thickness. Like silk. What would the rest of her feel like if he dared touch her?

What was he thinking? It would be bad enough at any other time, imagining her as a woman and not only an off-limits witch, but now? Fatigue, hunger, frustration. They must've been to blame. His brain had to settle on something that had nothing to do with Derek and his crazy friends. The cute witch leaning against him was as good a distraction as any.

The snow slowed a bit at a time. Micah guessed they'd hiked a few miles by the time it came to a stop. "Oh, no." Esme stopped, her breath coming in hitching little gasps as she looked around, then overhead. "It's not snowing anymore."

"Don't worry about it." He could worry enough for the both of them. "There's no wind, so that helps, too. Our scent won't carry as far or as easily."

He took a deep breath, closing his eyes to sharpen his sense of smell. "For what it's worth, I can't pick up their scent. Any of them. We're okay." *For now. We're okay for now.* He didn't dare say that.

He didn't think he needed to, either. She was stubborn, and stupid enough to curse a bunch of shifters, but she wasn't entirely brainless.

At least the position of the stars told him they were moving in the right direction. "We're on the right path. Come on. We should keep moving." She nodded, her expression hardening into something that screamed determination, and he couldn't help but like her even more than before.

He did like her. That was the most unpredictable part of this. They bickered, they found ways to get under each other's skin. He wanted to strangle her sometimes. But he liked her. She was strong, she was determined. She wouldn't break down even now, when a breakdown might be the best thing for both of them. At least then she might go along with him when he picked her up and carried her to safety. She might not be so determined to put up a fight.

"I didn't think it would drive him to this point."

He looked down at her, startled. She hadn't said much until then, and usually in response to something he'd said. "What?"

"Derek. All of them. I admit, I didn't know it would go this far."

He barely managed to suppress anger. "You cast a curse without knowing where it would end up?"

"It's not like baking a cake."

"So why do it?"

She grunted, though that could've been as much from exertion as anything else. "You wouldn't understand."

"That's a cowardly thing to say."

"Cowardly?" She stopped, planting her feet, and he regretted it.

"Come on. I shouldn't have said that. We have to keep moving." When she only glared up at him, eyes flashing in the darkness, he growled. "It's up to you. I'll leave you here to deal with whatever comes next. I don't need to risk my neck for you."

"Then why are you doing it? Why did you do any of this?"

Good question. He never did give her a full answer when she'd asked before this, either. When she'd demanded to know why he rescued her.

"Can we at least keep moving while I explain? Or would you rather make it easier for them to find us?" She rolled her eyes but took his arm, leaning against him as they started off again. "I don't think it's a secret that I don't agree with the curse."

"No, really?"

"Could you please put a stopper in it for a minute while I answer your questions?" She blew out an exasperated sigh but didn't say anything. "Like I said, I don't agree with it. I think it's a shady, sneaky thing to do. But I don't believe you should be, you know. Executed for it."

"Thanks." There was no bitterness or sarcasm in that. It was the faintest whisper.

"You should at least get a trial or something before anyone decides whether you should be punished."

"Are you serious? I should be tried?" Her fingers dug into his arm. He barely felt it, though he suspected she was squeezing as hard as she could.

"You did something wrong. I'm only a shifter, but even I know that. You cursed shifters and separated them from their wolves. It's driving them out of their minds. That's not the kind of thing a person—a witch—gets away with. Not until they at least plead their case in front of a council. Some kind of ruling body."

He stepped over a boulder and reached out to help her. She hesitated. "So it's not because you agree with what I did. It's because you think I should be able to defend myself before I face punishment."

"In a word, yes." He kept his arms outstretched. "Come on."

She didn't move. Her eyes never left his face. "What if I told you I already tried to get justice? Years ago. And nobody listened to me. What about that?"

"What?" He lowered his arms. "What are you talking about? Years ago? I thought this all started with your friend."

"I wish it had." She snickered, tipping her head back to look up at the stars. "I really wish it had."

"Come on. We can't keep stopping like this." He took her hand, tried to be as gentle as he could while also trying to get the urgency of the situation through to her. Why was she having such a hard time understanding?

"I'm going to have to sit down soon. I'm going to have to rest."

"I know that." He did, though he was doing everything he could to keep that from happening. "Which is why I should be carrying you."

"No, thanks." Now she was nasty, her nose wrinkling. "I don't want a shifter who isn't on my side carrying me anywhere. How do I know you'd let go before we got to Jordan Greystone's compound?"

It was his turn to be offended. "After what I've already put myself through for you? You think I'd betray you like that?"

She let out a long breath before shrugging. "How do I know?"

"I guess you don't, do you?" He looked her up and down, then took a slow look around at their surroundings. "Are you ready to take a chance? Getting home without me, I mean?"

There was a long moment when neither of them

spoke. The air between them seemed to crackle—maybe her magic was starting to come back. And maybe it wasn't a good idea to push her any further. She might set him on fire without meaning to, angry as she was.

"Fine." She reached for him, and they started off again. Much to his chagrin, they were moving even slower than before. Every step pained her. As frustrated as he was, he felt sorry for her. Why did she insist on torturing herself?

They walked on, the woods silent. The way they always were after a snowfall. It was almost religious, or as close to a religious experience as Micah had ever or would ever experience. Sacred silence.

Silence Esme broke into. "I hate him. That's why I did it. Not only because of what he's still doing. Because I hate him for what he did to me."

"Derek."

She nodded.

"He did something to you?"

Another nod.

"Before tonight?"

"Yes, yes, of course. Before tonight." There was pain and fatigue in her voice. "Long before tonight."

"What happened?" She shook her head this time, looking down at the ground. At their feet, plodding so slowly. "What, you still don't think you can trust me? Believe me. No love lost between me and any of that pack."

"What difference does it make? In the end, you all protect each other. This pack, that pack, it doesn't matter."

Now he was the one who wanted to stop dead where they stood. "How can you say that? You don't know me."

"I know your kind."

"Oh, I see. That's how it is."

"Get real, Micah. Don't tell me you don't feel exactly the same about witches."

"You don't know how I feel." When she snickered, it angered him worse than ever. "You don't. Even if you did, you wouldn't know why. Just like I don't know why you'd be stupid enough to cast a curse on the alpha's son. I mean, how idiotic do you have to be?"

"Idiotic?" She snickered again, gripping his arm harder than she needed to. "You're lucky my powers are taking a break or whatever they're doing. I'd make you regret that."

"Yeah, I'm shaking."

"No. I'm shaking, because I'm freezing half to death." She looked up at him. "You want to know?

Do you really want to know why I cursed him? Why I hate him and wish he was never born? Do you want to hear about it? Because once you do, you might end up feeling conflicted. I wouldn't want to knock you off your high horse."

She was one to talk about high horses. "Be my guest. Open my mind, Esme. Tell me why you pulled a move like this, when you had to know the consequences would be pretty severe."

Her arm tightened around his, though he didn't know if that was indignation or a desperate attempt at staying on her feet. "Did you bring the bracelet with you?"

A strange question. "I didn't think it'd be safe to leave it in that shack, where they might find it when they're searching."

"What if I told you I was the first witch who ever wore one of them?"

10

That got him. Just like she knew it would.

He almost lost his footing, too busy staring down at her to watch where he was going. Once he found his balance, he let out a pained sound. "You? Tonight wasn't the first time?"

"No. It wasn't. Though the bracelet itself has changed. Back then, it was more of a cuff than a chain." She chuckled, then wondered why she had. Exhaustion and pain and weakness, and the sense of touching the surface of her most painful memory were doing things to her mind. Making her react in strange ways. "I guess technology has improved or something."

"When was this?"

"Years ago. Four— No, five this spring. It's hard to believe it's been that long. Sometimes it feels like yesterday. Other times it feels like another lifetime. I can hardly remember that version of me. That version of my life."

She was making him uncomfortable. It rolled off him in waves, and she wondered if this was her magic coming back. Sensing his inner feelings. It gave her hope, though she knew darn well anybody would be uncomfortable with the direction her story had already taken. Nobody started off that way when there was a happy ending ahead.

"It's funny. Not ha-ha funny. Strange, I guess. That's a better word." She sucked in a pained gasp when she stumbled over a snow-covered rock. Amazing the way the muscles and joints all worked together. When a person was healthy, whole, they didn't need to give a moment's thought to that inter-play. That seamless functioning.

Now? It was another story. Now she felt every twitch, every stretch.

"What's strange?"

"Sylvia's spent all these years trying to get me to open up about it. What happened. She knows— plenty of witches do. Shifters, too, though not your pack. They wouldn't have let word get out. Always protecting the black sheep of the family."

"You're losing me."

"Sorry. My mind's wandering." Her mind was broken. That was the problem. She needed rest and lots of it, but that wasn't happening. Not right now. "Anyway, Sylvia's tried to drag it out of me more times than I want to remember. But here I am, ready to tell you the whole story."

"It could be because we aren't close. It's easier to talk to a stranger."

"You're probably right." Of all strangers, it would have to be him, wouldn't it? "Well, suffice it to say Derek tested out his little toy on me. Before that, we were engaged."

"No kidding. Seriously?"

"What? You think nobody would ever want to marry me?"

"I mean... it's not usually like that. We don't do the dating-engagement-marriage thing. We find our mates, and then we go through all that human stuff for the sake of making it legal or whatever."

"But it's not always like that, is it? He told me so, anyway."

Micah was quiet for a while, concentrating on

his footing as they crossed what used to be a stream but was now barely a trickle. The banks were just as treacherous, though. I wasn't until they were across, with her breath coming in sharp gasps, that he responded. "I guess it can happen the way you described. A shifter and a witch fall in love or what have you and get engaged. I can't imagine anybody falling in love with him, though."

"I agree. It's hard to imagine. I don't know what I was thinking." She tried to laugh it off, but she didn't have the strength. "He was different then, or at least that was what I told myself. That he was special, you know? And he does have charisma to spare. He's charming when he wants to be. Passionate, too."

"I don't need to hear any more of that, thanks. I don't enjoy thinking about Derek in the first place, without his passions coming into it."

"Fair enough. Anyway, I was an idiot. Just like you said before. I fooled myself into believing we'd make it work. Coming from different backgrounds, you know. Then there's the whole thing about his father wanting to wipe witches from the face of the earth."

"I can imagine that would put a damper on things. You didn't think that would be a problem?"

She gave the question serious thought. It seemed like the fair thing to do after he went to all this trouble. "You know, it's a powerful thing. Intoxicating."

"What is?"

"The idea of somebody caring more about you and what you have together than they do about their lineage. Their family. Their entire pack. He put me on a pedestal and swore I was the only thing in the world that mattered." Even now, with years of understanding between then and now, she couldn't help remembering that feeling. Like she was that important, that necessary to someone. Nothing mattered as much as she did.

"So something happened to throw all of that out of whack." She nodded slowly. "What was it?"

"Derek being himself. He was only being who he was—and no, I'm not defending him if that's what you think. There's no defense for what he's done. For who he is."

"What did he do?"

"He cheated on me." She snorted. "It must sound ridiculous. Of course, he was going to cheat on me. It's who he is. He can't be bothered to tie himself down to one person. Not the alpha's son. He's too special for that."

"I'm sorry."

"Don't be." She looked up at him. "Don't. Because it needed to happen. I needed something strong enough to shake me out of the... I don't know what to call it. Self-hypnosis, maybe. Whatever spell I put myself under to make myself believe he was better than he is."

He chuckled, and it wasn't without warmth or understanding. "I'd bet you didn't feel that way at the time."

"No." They shared a quiet, regretful little laugh. "No, I didn't take that attitude at the time. I lost it. Blew up. He broke my heart. It finally occurred to me that it probably wasn't even the first time. It almost never is, you know? By the time a person finds out, I mean."

"I understand what you mean. So what did you do once you absorbed the shock?"

"I broke up with him in front of his entire pack."

"You did?" When she nodded, he whistled softly. "Wow. That took guts."

"It took something, all right. I don't know if it was guts, though. Fury, maybe. Rage. Humiliation. I wanted to humiliate him the way he'd done to me. I wanted everybody in his pack to know what a lying, cheating, sniveling little nothing he was."

After a moment, he grunted. "I would've wanted the same thing."

"Only it backfired on me. Big time."

"I'm almost afraid to ask how."

"You already know the basics. The bracelet. As soon as Amy mentioned it, it's like I was right back there. Like years had melted away, and I was back in that nightmare." She drew as deep a breath as she could manage without hurting herself too badly. "That's how I knew it was him. I mean, I would've guessed it anyway, but the bracelet drove it home."

She sensed his hesitation. Discomfort. No one liked hearing about things like this, of course. She'd feel just as uncomfortable if the situation was reversed and Micah wanted to tell her all about the most traumatic experience of his life. It wouldn't mean her wishing he'd keep it to himself—not at all. She wouldn't know how to react. How to respond. Whether she should offer comfort.

Especially considering their prickly relationship. The way they seemed to excel at irritating each other. Even a well-intended comment might be taken the wrong way.

He stayed silent. She appreciated that. No empty platitudes.

"He waited until the next full moon." The moon's

light on the fallen snow reminded her of it, even if her reckoning had taken place in spring. "It was two weeks after I embarrassed him in front of the pack. I was naïve enough to think it was all over. Like he was capable of moving on without making sure to get the last laugh."

Her foot slipped, and she almost fell, but Micah caught her. And that was nice. For a second, she felt safe and protected, and the warmth from his body was almost enough to make her lean into him not for support, but for comfort. That was all wrong. She straightened herself, keeping her eyes low. "He came to my house. I didn't spend so much time there back then. I was usually out doing things. With friends, with Sylvia, that sort of stuff. When Derek got there, I was making candles, the way I always do at the full moon. He knew that. He knew I'd be there."

Sickness washed over her, but it wasn't anything to do with her wound or exhaustion or fear. It was memory. So clear and crisp. "I knew right away he wasn't there to make up or apologize. He knocked me out, carried me away. I came to the way I did tonight. Tied to a tree. Unable to use my powers because of the bracelet on my wrist."

It was getting harder to speak. Harder to move. Her very muscles were freezing—at least, that was how it felt. Her joints ached from the cold and damp. Her feet might as well have not been attached to her ankles. Was this how it felt to be human? Powerless, defenseless against the elements?

"It took three days."

Micah grunted. "Three days?"

"Yes. I was out there in the woods for three days while Derek and his buddies tortured me." Now she might as well have been talking about somebody else. Her insides were as numb as the rest of her. That was for the best, really, and she knew it. The detachment protected her. "For a while, they left me tied to the tree and messed with my head. They blindfolded me, sneaked around, slapped at me with branches and belts. Their hands. Then their fists."

"Ah, Esme." His voice was heavy with sorrow.

Now there was no stopping. The dam was broken, and everything had to come out. "Then they set me loose, but I was still wearing the bracelet, so I couldn't use my powers. They chased me, hunted me. I was disoriented and exhausted, and starving. Terrified."

Silence fell between them, broken only by their feet crunching the snow and her occasional hissing intakes of breath. The pain was only worsening, strong and sharp enough to make her wish she could scream. How much longer would it be before they reached safety?

"I guess they got bored." Even her voice was weak, but she had to hold on. Had to make him understand. "He took the bracelet off, finally, after catching me. I was sure he'd kill me, but all he did was smirk down at me. Curled up on the ground, begging him to stop what he was doing. He left me there, but I managed to find my way home once my head cleared and my magic returned."

The next memory brought a bitter taste to her mouth. "Then, I made the mistake of thinking there would be justice for what I went through. I took a day to rest and clean myself up. Then, I went to Jordan."

"That was brave. Especially after what you went through."

"It was pointless. A waste of time."

"You mean, you told him—"

"And he didn't care. That's exactly what happened." Bitterness leaked into her voice, but then it would. "He told me it was my word against his son's, and his son was hunting with the pack during the moon. I was still bruised and scraped, and there was a mark around my wrist from the bracelet. You know what he said?"

She snorted at the memory, Jordan's cold voice ringing out in her head. "I don't know what you witches get up to in your free time. Don't blame your rituals on anyone of my bloodline."

A wolf growled. No, it was Micah who did it, Micah who bared his teeth in a snarl. "That sounds like him. He could be here with us now, even."

"So there you have it. No justice. No closure for me. Sylvia would tell you I've become a recluse and run away from the world. Maybe she's right." Her voice tightened, trembling. "But what am I supposed to do? Risk running into him? Into any of them? So they can laugh and sneer and know they got away with what they did?"

They came to a stop, and she was glad for the chance to catch her breath. Micah turned to her, wrapping an arm around her, holding her upright. Keeping her close. Warm.

He touched her cheek, and that was warm, too. She resisted the yearning to lean into his touch, to ask for more. What a mixed blessing this was. His nearness. "I'm sorry about all of it."

"Thank you."

"And I understand why you did it. I can't even blame you anymore."

Another blessing. She closed her eyes, willing

herself not to cry but failing when a tear leaked out anyway.

"And I promise you." There was a growl under his words, dancing on the edge of his voice. "I'm going to get you to safety. You'll be safe with my pack. And we'll make sure nothing happens to you."

11

Micah had to get her home.

"Are you sure this is safe?" Esme grunted as they worked together to lower her onto a flat rock at the base of an old, gnarled tree. Its branches stretched out far, the oldest limbs thicker than Micah's thighs, some of them arching away from the trunk and touching the stony ground. They provided something of a shelter against the slowly strengthening wind.

Once she was finished resting, he'd insist on carrying her the rest of the way. It was too cold. Too wet. She'd end up with pneumonia before long, and without her powers he wondered how she'd fare against it. Whether she'd be strong enough to fight it off.

Why was that his problem? Why was any of this his problem?

Because he'd stepped up. He'd put himself in the center of this. For better or worse, he didn't know. He only knew he couldn't abandon her now.

"Safe or not, you need to rest. And the air's clear. No sign of any of them." That couldn't possibly last long, but he wouldn't say it out loud. He doubted there was a need to. She was tired, not feebleminded.

"How's this treating you?" He lifted her sweater, leaning in close so his body heat would comfort her, then carefully peeled away her makeshift bandage. The tank was ruined, but then it already had been. The new blood staining the cloth was what worried him now. That and the worsening conditions underneath.

"Oh…" That was all she managed as they both looked down at her side. How was it possible? The wound couldn't be more than hours old—it was nowhere near dawn yet—but it looked like it was beginning to fester. There was pus and an unpleasant odor coming from it.

Once again, the sense that he was in over his head threatened to make Micah roar. How was he supposed to get them out of this when he couldn't get a grip on what they were up against?

"How is it possible?" Esme's voice shook. "Unless the dagger he used had magic, too. Like the bracelets."

"So you think he used something he knew would poison you? Is that what you mean?"

"Exactly. Why else would it be festering already?" She squeezed her eyes shut, and the expression went straight to his chest, tightening it. Stirring up a fire in there, the sort of fire that could easily become an inferno. How could Derek do this? To her or to anyone? Who did he think he was?

When this was over, and Esme was safe, he'd make sure Derek paid for everything he'd done. No matter what it took.

He lowered her sweater before sitting beside her. She nestled against him without a word, and he accepted that, welcomed it. She needed his warmth. Her trembling lessened, and her teeth eventually stopped chattering. "That's one good thing about shifters. You're so warm."

He stifled his laughter for the sake of keeping their location secret. "I'm glad it's coming in handy for you. At least I'm doing one thing right."

"You've done more than one thing right." She lowered her head to his shoulder. "Thank you for listening to me. For believing me. Whatever happens, I want you to know that means everything."

"Nothing's going to happen besides getting you to safety. You're going to be okay." He found her hand, tucked into the crook of his elbow, and closed his fingers around it. "You're going to be fine."

She only let out a tiny sigh. "I just want it to be over. I'm so tired."

"You'll feel better once you've rested." Empty words, hollow. He didn't even believe them. Why did he feel compelled to say them? Why did people do anything in emergencies? A desperate scramble to make sense of situations that defied logic.

He wasn't accustomed to this. Knowing there were forces at work outside his control.

"I'm sure you're right." And if she was so quick to agree with him, she had to be in worse shape than she was letting on. He admired her courage even if she still struck him as being too hardheaded.

He kept his focus on the wind, the air around them, searching for signs of Derek or the others. There was nothing on the air but the clean smell of snow. Wet leaves, wet needles.

"How close do you think they are?" Her voice

sounded far away. Sleepy. He wasn't sure if it was a good idea to let her fall asleep. The cold affected her so much more than it did him. Would she freeze?

"I wish I knew." He looked down at her, chuckling softly. Ruefully. "Sorry. I know that doesn't help."

"No, it doesn't." She chuckled. "It's okay. I only wanted to talk. To keep talking. It's better than thinking, you know?"

Yes, and he had probably done her a big favor by listening to her story earlier. Not only because she deserved to have somebody listen, though that was important. He sensed her relief, felt it. Giving her something to focus on beyond their predicament—and her pain—was just as crucial.

He'd do that for her again. And for himself, since thinking about Derek only made him want more and more to break free of Esme and do a little hunting of his own. The wolf snarled in his mind, hungry for blood.

"Let's talk, then. What do you want to talk about?"

She lifted a shoulder. "I don't know. What about you? Tell me something about you. What do you do when you're not rescuing witches in distress?"

He snickered, wrapping his arms around her.

She sighed, a happy little noise, and he was glad he'd done it. "I like aggravating witches, too. I'm pretty good at that."

"No comment."

He grinned down at the top of her head. "I mean, there's not much to do. Not much we have to do. Our ancestors, the pack elders and the ones who came before them, saw to it the pack never had to want for much of anything. They invested gold, purchased huge tracts of land. Commercial real estate. Everything was sort of lumped together in a pot, and the returns provide for us."

"So you don't work?"

"Do you?"

"We aren't talking about me." She wasn't sharp about it, though, but rather gentle. "For what it's worth, it's similar for us. My parents made sure I was provided for, the way theirs did for them. I could work if I wanted to, though. Sylvia once had an idea about me opening a store next to hers."

"Really? What would you sell?"

"Tonics. Ointments. Candles, crystals, that sort of thing. Humans are into that sort of stuff now, which is funny when you think about it. Back in the day, witches were hunted and tortured, and murdered. Now? It's trendy to own a deck of tarot cards."

"I think that's a good idea."

"No, you don't." She snickered, lifting her head to look up at him. "You're only saying that."

"I'm not. I think it would be good for you to have that. You can't be happy, living all alone the way you do. It must get lonely."

She stiffened a little in his arms, and he knew he'd said the wrong thing. "I don't mind. I actually like it."

"But it's not because you want things to be that way. You felt like there was no other choice after what happened to you. You said it yourself, Sylvia thinks—"

"I know what Sylvia thinks. I know what you probably think. I have my reasons."

"I believe you." It was easier than arguing, which was a waste of time. A waste of Esme's strength, too.

"What about you?"

"Me?"

She nodded, her head rubbing against his shoulder. "You. You live alone?"

"As alone as someone can be when they have a pack around them all the time."

"But you don't live in a commune. Even I know that. Your houses are close together. You're sort of a neighborhood. But that's not the same as living with someone."

He didn't have it in him to tell her she was wrong. It would be an empty lie, anyway. "What makes you say all of this? Have you been thinking about me?" He was trying to tease her, to get her off the topic. It made him uncomfortable, talking about himself this way. He wasn't used to talking about his life.

"Do you want me to think about you?" So she still had it in her to throw sarcastic little comments around. A good sign. "If you're interested in the truth, I'll tell you. I felt it in you when we were together at Ezra's. When he was going through his problems."

"You felt it in me? Felt what?"

She sighed, and for a moment, he thought she might be too weak to answer. He didn't know whether it would be a good thing or not, her never answering his question. Did he want to know, really? Could he stand not knowing?

What did she know about him?

What if—

"Loneliness. I felt how lonely you are. You put on this mask for the rest of the world. You joke around and act like you don't take things very seriously, but your energy told a different story. And it didn't feel much different when you visited my cabin."

"You think I'm lonely?"

"Micah, I know you are." She lifted her head, half-lidded eyes meeting his. "You don't have to pretend. There's no use in it, anyway. I can see through you."

Evidently, she couldn't see as much as she thought she did if the only thing she'd come back with was his loneliness. He supposed he should be grateful for that. "I guess I am, but it's not a bad thing. I've always done better on my own."

"Always?" She lifted an eyebrow before her head fell against his shoulder again.

"Okay. Maybe not always."

"Who was she?" She must've heard his sharp intake of breath, because she chuckled. "Come on. You can't lie to me. I'm a living, breathing lie detector."

She'd be a lot of fun to live with, wouldn't she? He wouldn't be able to get a single thing past her. "Marsha. Her name is Marsha. We were pretty serious for a while. It's been a long time since we broke up." Strange how the mention of her name didn't bother him the way it used to. He could barely remember why seeing her at Jordan's had affected him like it did. Why did he care?

"Marsha. The name is familiar. Uncommon nowadays." She gasped. "Isn't she—"

"She's from Jordan's pack, yeah."

"That's right. I heard she was dating someone outside the pack. So that was you."

"Not for too long, but yes. It was me."

"You broke up ages ago, though, didn't you?" He grunted his affirmation. "And there hasn't been anyone since?"

There were limits to what he was willing to go through for the sake of distracting her. "Guess who she's with now?"

"Oh, no. You're kidding."

"I wish I was." He snorted, scowling into the darkness. "They're perfect for each other."

"She must've really hurt you. I wouldn't wish Derek on anybody."

Red flags popped up in his head. He had already said too much. "I'd rather not talk about it anymore."

"It's okay. I'm not trying to pry." She shifted a little, making herself more comfortable. He doubted it made much of a difference. "It's just that I'm sorry you're alone, and that you feel sad."

"I don't need pity."

"Good, because I don't pity you. If it's pity you're looking for, keep looking."

It was absurd, laughing at a time like this, but he couldn't help it. Even now, when there was so much at stake. She was like a breath of fresh air. "I'll keep that in mind."

She wasn't like anybody he'd ever known. Shifter, witch, it didn't matter. There was something different about her. He could relate to her, could be honest with her. She wouldn't judge him. And yes, her stubbornness was a problem, but he couldn't even fault her for that. He was stubborn, too. He hated accepting help, hated thinking he might look weak if he admitted needing it.

And maybe that had resulted in him being lonely. Sad. It wasn't until Esme pointed it out that he ever acknowledged his loneliness. He didn't even mind her sensing it in him. Not really.

She saw him. She knew him. And she had shared something with him that she hadn't even shared with her cousin. Because she felt as comfortable with him as he did with her.

Or was he kidding himself?

Just then, he couldn't bring himself to care much. Not when she was in his arms, trusting and needing him. He held her closer, as tight as he dared. The small sigh of comfort and trust that resulted warmed his chest, made his heart swell.

Made him hook a finger under her chin and lift it until he could look into her eyes. Until he could lower his head and press his lips to hers the way he had back at the shack, when she'd first woken up. This wasn't the same thing, not by a long shot. He wasn't giving in to a moment of madness. Weakness.

He was doing this with a clear head. Kissing the witch—the woman—he wanted to know better. He wanted to know everything about her.

When she leaned into his kiss and curled a hand at the base of his neck, he knew he wasn't alone in this. It was more than the heat of the moment. Something in her fit against something in him the way her body fit against his now, curled up against him while they sat on this rock. The cold, the dampness in the air, none of that mattered now that she was in his arms and wanting him the way he and his wolf wanted her.

Still, there was one misgiving teasing its way across the back of his mind. "You're hurt." He managed it between kisses pressed against her lips, her chin, her cheek. Her skin was so sweet, so soft. If he tasted every inch, it wouldn't be enough. He could've spent hours soaking her in, memorizing her.

"Just kiss me." She placed a hand against his jaw and turned his head until their lips met again. Desire surged inside him, and in spite of wanting to protect and shelter her, his need for her was stronger. His need for connection with this brave, headstrong, maddening woman.

But she was weak. Exhausted. Sick. He had to settle for a few more stolen kisses, for the thrill of having her in his arms with her heartbeat running through his head. Stronger, quicker, beating the way his did. "You should get some more rest." He kissed the tip of her nose. Her forehead. If Derek put a hand on her, he'd kill him. As simple as that.

"We have to keep going, though, don't we?" Her cheeks were pink, her eyes brighter than before. She stroked his hair, a faint smile tipping her lips at the corners. The sort of smile people exchanged after crossing the line, after getting to know each other in a way they hadn't before. He loved the sight of it, what it meant.

Even if he couldn't give himself over to it. He hated Derek for that, too.

Though if it wasn't for his attack, would they have the opportunity to share this moment?

"Close your eyes." He stroked her hair before pulling her head to his shoulder. "Just rest, okay? You don't need to think about anything else right now. Get your strength back. I won't let anybody hurt you."

"I know you won't." Her voice was already fainter. Thick with sleep. She must've fought hard to stay away as long as she had. His heart swelled again with admiration. She was so brave.

He leaned against the trunk at his back, letting his head rest against the bark. Maybe it was the hours of exertion or the energy he'd expended caring for Esme, but he was suddenly tired. It took a lot to wear out a shifter. Leave it to Esme to be the one to manage it.

He allowed his eyes to close, telling himself he was no good to her unless he got a little sleep, too. She was warm now, comfortable, and far away in some dream world. They'd be fine.

And they were.

Until a familiar scent announced itself.

His eyes snapped open. The position of the stars and moon told him it couldn't have been more than an hour since he'd fallen asleep. The wind had picked up, coming from the east.

And on it was Derek's scent.

"Esme. Esme, wake up." For one brief, terrifying moment, he thought she wouldn't. That she'd slipped away while he slept and allowed it to happen. He shook her hard enough to make her head drop from his shoulder—but it woke her. "Come on. We need to go right now."

"Is it him?" She was still half-asleep. He pulled her to her feet, hating that he had to do it but knowing it was necessary.

"Yes, he's somewhere close. Let's move."

And to his relief, she was stronger than before. Faster.

For now, at least.

12

"How's this for irony?" Micah extended his arm for Esme to lean on as they crossed another creek. "There I was, determined to carry you, but I didn't think about how slick the ground is. It would be one thing for me to lose my balance when I'm moving fast, but I wouldn't want to do it while I'm holding you."

"See? Turns out I have instincts, too." Not that her instincts had anything to do with her refusing his help. In fact, now she wished he would carry her. Every step was agony, and the wound was warmer all the time. She knew that was a bad sign, that infection was spreading. If only she knew the nature of the infection. What sort of dark magic was in that dagger? How would it affect her?

Was it the reason she still couldn't use her magic? Because no matter how she tried, nothing seemed to work. She would focus her attention on a patch of ground and send warmth in that direction, holding up a hand in expectation of a ball of light that never came. She couldn't even melt a patch of snow, one of the most basic things a witch was capable of.

"I'll tell you one thing." Even talking wiped her out, but silence was worse. If she wasn't talking, the pain was too noticeable. "I've learned a lesson. No more misusing magic."

"I don't know." Micah grunted, a surly sound that paired well with his lowered brow. "I'm starting to wonder if you misused it or not."

"Goodness. Are you actually on my side?" She was trying to joke, trying to lighten the mood, but one look in his eyes told her it was a waste of time. Wasted effort, too, and she was so weak already.

"Of course, I'm on your side." He held her with a firm arm, keeping her close to him. Somehow that convinced her more than his words did. He really did believe her. He was on her side. The first shifter who'd taken her seriously, since Jordan certainly hadn't.

If only that did anything for pain. Not to mention

the uncomfortable warmth she was now experiencing. To think, she had been so cold in the first hours of their hike through the snow. Now she felt flushed all over, so much so that she considered taking off her sweater. No matter how tempting the idea was, she still had enough sense to know it would be a mistake.

Besides, Micah would never let her get away with it. To think, there was somebody with her best interests at heart. Somebody wanted to take care of her. It had been so long—since before she'd met Derek, easily. He had never wanted to take care of her. She knew that now, thanks to the firm arm around her waist and the memory of Micah's kisses.

Excellent kisses. The sort of kisses that could easily have led to more if it weren't for their location and the situation they were in. Maybe that was for the best. There was nothing so awkward as a regretful morning after. She hadn't exactly made a hobby of those mornings, but she had known a few of them.

Somehow, it would be worse with Micah. Because she did like him. This was more than wanting somebody and then forgetting all about it once the moment passed. There was more than that between them. Something real, maybe.

Then again, she was flushed with fever, so what did she know? Once she was better, she could feel differently about him. She probably would, too. And that would be for the best. She sure hadn't made any friends among shifters, performing that curse.

If anything, it would be easier for Micah if this was all nothing but a memory.

"Ow." She winced, bending a little, struggling to catch her breath after a sharp, shooting pain knocked the wind out of her lungs.

He hovered over her, eager to do anything she needed. "It's getting worse."

She wanted to argue with them, at least to ease his mind a little, but there was no use. This wasn't a fairytale. They wouldn't get anywhere with lies, even if the lies had good intentions behind them. "I think it is. I don't think I'm going to make it."

"Don't talk like that. We haven't come all this way to give up now." The sky was starting to lighten, telling her they'd walked for hours. Micah looked up, looked around, then pointed to a ridge up ahead. "Once we hit that, we'll be able to see the valley. I bet there isn't more than a couple of miles left to go."

She wanted to believe him. She wanted so badly, as much as she wanted to throw her arms around him and beg him not to leave her. Everything was so mixed up, fever wiping away her good sense. "Maybe you should run ahead and see, then come back. I'll wait here."

"Esme, no."

"I'm only slowing you down. What's the point of both of us getting caught, anyway?" She reached out, touching her palm to his cheek. There was almost no difference in temperature between her skin and his, telling her she was getting sicker. "Go ahead. I'll wait. Where else am I going to go?"

"I won't have you talk that way." He wedged his shoulder under her arm, practically lifting her off her feet. "Come on. We don't have much further." She didn't have it in her to tell him how much it hurt, being held this way. What did comfort matter now? She would either be killed once Derek caught her, or she would die from whatever was burning its way through her system.

At least she knew this in her final hours. Connection. Touch. Comfort.

"You're going to be fine." He grunted through clenched teeth, dragging both of them up the incline leading to the ridge. The ground was rocky, slick thanks to the snow, making it slow going.

"You could move so much faster without me."

"Would you stop that?" He sounded sharp, angry.

She would have, too, in his situation. He was frustrated. He wanted so much to be the hero, to save her.

"But if they catch up to us, they'll hurt you." Tears blurred her vision at the thought of him being under attack, especially because of her. He didn't deserve that.

"I don't want to hear about it." He reached out with his free hand, taking hold of a thick tree limb and using it to pull them further up the slope. "Just try to do your best to work with me. That's all I'm asking. And hold on." She did her best, the way he asked.

She heard them before she saw them.

Even if she hadn't heard them, if they moved silently, she would've felt the change in Micah and known what it meant. He froze, a growl rumbling in his chest. And she knew.

It all happened so fast.

One second, she was in Micah's arms. The next, she was loose, tumbling down the rocky slope they had just climbed. Somewhere in the middle of the pain—agonizing, blazing pain—she heard Micah's voice as he cried out for her.

She came to a stop, finally, staring up at the sky. It was almost dawn. Her breath came back to her, and she tried to sit up, biting the inside of her cheek against a scream. She had reopened the wound, and blood now flowed from it.

Above, the shifters taunted Micah, cackling wildly. "Did you lose your girlfriend?" One of them lunged at Micah, who backed away, scrambling to keep his feet while loose rocks rolled away.

Why wasn't he shifting? Then it occurred to her. They were still outside his pack's territory. Maybe he couldn't shift here. No, he'd been his wolf when he found her last night. Maybe he had to perform the shift in his own territory. Her brain was barely working as it was thanks to her fever, and now she had terror to contend with.

All she knew for sure was this: they were desperately outnumbered, and Micah would worry more about her than about himself.

"Don't worry, we'll deal with her." Derek laughed, watching the way Esme did as three of the shifters lunged at Micah as one, overwhelming him. She didn't have the strength to scream for him, just like she couldn't scream when one of them picked up a rock and threw it at the back of Micah's head.

It was like watching someone fall in slow motion. He landed on his back, his face turned toward her, and a thin trickle of blood began running down the side of his neck.

"That was almost too easy." Derek was triumphant, standing at the top of the ridge, now looking around to see where Esme had landed. For a second, she thought she might be able to hide, but she understood the flaw in that plan before she could move.

She was bleeding. He could smell her.

"I found you!" He practically sang it, sounding happier than she'd ever heard him. It was sick, twisted, insane. She tried to back away, crab walking on her hands and feet while the group of them laughed and mocked her.

"Come on, Esme. You should know me better than that." Derek took his time, sauntering down the slope, rocks skittering away with each step. "I don't give up once I set my sights on something. Remember?"

"You realize the entire Shotgun Falls pack is going to come after you for this." It was a stupid, weak threat, but that was all she had. Threats. Feeble promises. Her eyes darted back and forth, taking in the sight of the snarling, sweating, crazed shifters now surrounding her.

Maybe it was knowing these were probably her

final moments. Somehow she managed to transcend the pain, pushing it deep down in favor of getting on her feet. If she was going to die, she wouldn't do it begging. She would be on her feet.

And while she was at it, she would carry a rock. Why not? They were all over the place. She could at least hurt him before he did what he was going to do.

Derek saw it, then burst out laughing. "What do you think you're going to do with that? You might have made it so I can't shift, but come on. Do you think that will have any effect coming from you?" When one of his friends advanced on her, he held up a hand. "No. She's mine. Just like we talked about."

"You realize if you kill me, you'll never know how to lift the curse. I tried telling you last night, but you didn't want to hear it then, either."

"You didn't tell me anything but lies." His eyes were flat, lifeless, with dark circles already forming underneath them. His friends didn't look much better. How long could a shifter live without their wolf?

"I was telling the truth."

"Then that's fine." He shrugged, grinning, turning her blood to ice. "If I'm the one who has to do it, I'll do it. Either way, you don't need to be breathing." A few of them laughed, but he didn't.

Her hand tightened around the rock. She was almost looking forward to using it.

He lunged.

Then bright, blue light blinded her. She dropped the rock, throwing an arm over her eyes, while the others let out shouts of surprise and confusion. When she lowered her arm, she found Derek sprawled on the ground, dazed.

She looked down at her hands. It hadn't come from her, that light. That burst of magic.

Her head snapped up in time to find Micah running for her. Of course, he wouldn't be down for long. Chaos erupted, with the other shifters closing in, standing between them.

Until Micah decided to unleash magic on them, too. He raised his hands, sending bursts of crackling light outward. The shifters fell, landing in a heap of arms and legs.

Magic. He had magic, too. This was no fever dream. "What—? How—?"

He didn't answer her unformed questions, gathering her in his arms, lifting her off the ground. He didn't say a word. He only took off running, bursting through the woods. All she could do was cling to him, burying her face in his shoulder, afraid now.

"You're dead! You're both dead!" She peered over Micah's shoulder, gasping when she caught sight of Derek and the others running full out. Chasing them, screaming and snarling. They couldn't shift, but they could run.

But Micah was faster. She looked up at him, found his eyes swirling with blue and amber light, the magic of witchcraft and shifter mixing together like cream in a cup of coffee. Only he was much more powerful. Did he know before now? Why didn't he tell her?

There was nothing to do but cling to him and hope he didn't drop her. At this speed, her body would be broken beyond repair. "Close. Close." It sounded like the wolf himself was speaking through Micah's mouth, and it scared her worse than ever. Like he was in a frenzy.

Finally, Micah slowed, his grip on her loosening a little. "We made it. We made it, we're safe." He was barely even winded, whereas Esme was on the verge of hyperventilating. Only once he set her on her feet could she breathe normally—even if every breath was still like a fresh stab wound to her side.

She was about to ask about his magic when

crashing noises behind them drew their attention. They turned, and Esme let out a strangled scream when Derek and the others burst out into the open. They were still coming. They didn't care about the border. "Stop!" Micah's voice was a roar, deep and commanding. "You're in Shotgun Falls territory now."

"Like I care." Derek charged straight at Micah, who pushed Esme behind him. She fell back, landing in the snow, watching with her heart in her throat as the two of them circled each other. The other shifters didn't bother coming for her. They were too busy staring at Micah, glaring at him, looking murderous while muttering obscenities and promising pain.

Relief washed over her when the shift started. The air around him vibrated, rippling like water. The rippling extended itself to his skin, his clothes. His body changed, lengthened, widened. A bright light emanated from him, the magic of the shift almost blinding her. She had never seen light like that coming from a shifter. But then he wasn't only a shifter, was he?

He fell on all fours, his growl filling her head and sending goosebumps racing up her arms. She wouldn't want him growling at her that way, but

Derek and his friends didn't seem to care much. They were too busy snarling, muttering curses and threats.

One of them lunged from behind, but Micah was quick, his wolf pivoting, his snapping jaws coming within inches of taking the shifter's hand. He did it again to another one, driving him back. Two of them approached, one from either side, and now it wasn't so easy. Who to drive back first? How many would lunge at him next?

They might not have been able to perform the shift themselves, but they were still strong. One of them kicked out, hitting Micah's left hind leg. He yelped, the leg going out from under him for a second, but he managed to recover quickly. Another one threw a rock at his head again. He ducked, but not fast enough, and now blood stained his tawny fur.

They were too much for him. He was outnumbered. Desperation rose in her chest, climbing into her throat, threatening to choke her. She had to do something. She couldn't let them outnumber him. She wouldn't watch him die.

All of it—the fear, the pain, the hate, the brief sense of connection with Micah, her panic. She drew it all together inside her, concentrating harder than she ever had since she'd first learned to harness her powers. *Please, don't abandon me now.* Would the goddess hear her? There was only one way to find out.

She raised her hands, holding them in front of her, focusing every ounce of what was left of her energy. "Micah! Move!"

Somehow he heard her, darting out of the way before she unleashed one single ball of light aimed straight at the six shifters before her.

At first, she wasn't sure she'd done anything. They could all move freely.

Until one of them tried to back away, outside the area he'd been standing in when she unleashed the spell. "What the...?" He raised his hands, feeling around in front of him, coming up against an invisible barrier. One by one, they realized they were trapped, all of them beating against the bars of the cage she'd closed around them.

Derek screamed, spit flying from his mouth when he did. "You'll pay for this! I'll make you pay if it's the last thing I ever do!" She believed he meant it, too.

More noise, this time coming from the other direction. A group of men—shifters, from the looks of them—flooded the clearing. She recognized one of them as Ezra and knew they were finally safe, for real this time. The Shotgun Falls pack had come to the rescue.

She didn't have it in her to check on Micah, to see if he was okay.

She couldn't do anything but fall back in the snow and let darkness overtake her.

13

The door to the bedroom opened, and Sylvia appeared. She held a finger to her lips as she closed the door, careful not to make a sound. Only once that was done did she say a word. "She's going to be fine."

Micah closed his eyes and let the words wash over him along with their meaning. Fine. Esme was going to be fine. He had done what he set out to do. He had kept them away from her. "Thank you."

He wasn't quite thanking Sylvia, even if he was grateful to her for treating her cousin's wounds. It was more of a prayer, or something close to it. Not that he ever prayed. Right now, though, it seemed like a good idea to start. Someone or something had guided them to safety, keeping them one step ahead of Derek and those crazed buddies of his.

Someone or something had kept Esme alive.

Sylvia smiled, placing a hand on his arm. He sensed her sympathy, and her gratitude. "The infection spread pretty aggressively, though. She will need a few days of rest while the magic works its way out of her system. It's a good thing I remembered how to make a poultice to pull out the infection." She motioned for him to follow her away from the bedroom. He didn't want to—even knowing she was on the mend, he didn't want to leave Esme's side.

Sher needed sleep more than anything else, though, and she wouldn't get it with him making conversation outside the bedroom. He followed Sylvia downstairs, to the kitchen. He'd never been in her home before and wasn't sure what to expect when she'd announced taking Esme there for treatment.

It wasn't much like Esme's, that was for sure. Sylvia lived a more modern life, her kitchen full of gadgets. "Do you want some coffee?" A touch of her hand to the refrigerator door turned on a light inside, giving them a look at the interior thanks to a clear glass door. "Hmm. I'm running low on creamer." She typed the word into a tablet mounted in the door, like a running grocery list.

When he thought about it, the whole setup made sense. She'd had her powers stripped away decades before then. This was as close to magic as she'd ever come. "No, thanks. I'm already jittery enough."

"You don't have any reason to be." She pulled out a bottled water, instead, tossing it to him. "You're dehydrated. I can tell. Drink up." Maybe she still held a little bit of magic, after all. Either that, or she used common sense. He'd described the hours they'd spent crossing into Shotgun Falls territory. It wasn't like they would've stopped off for something to eat and drink during that time.

"Did she wake up at all?" The water was a good move. The first sip left him craving more. Funny, but he hadn't felt thirsty before then. He was hungry, too, his stomach suddenly growling. Like he hadn't noticed any of his body's needs until then.

"Once or twice. Briefly."

"Did she say anything?"

If Sylvia heard the concern in his question, she was kind enough not to show it. Wise enough not to ask why he was so interested in what Esme had to say. "She asked if you were okay. I told her you were.

Then she asked where Derek was, and I told her he was locked up good and tight this time. He won't be escaping again." She smiled. "It did the trick. She was able to rest easier."

"I'm glad." Though that was only half the story. He was gladder she hadn't said anything about him. His use of magic. He hadn't known what he was doing, hadn't planned on any of it. It had never happened before, either. Not like that. Nothing that would knock full-grown shifters on their backs.

"It's a good thing she had you with her." Sylvia poured water from an electric kettle and dunked a tea bag in the mug before joining him at the table. "You were brave, going after her like that. All on your own, too."

"It felt like the right thing to do."

"I've always liked you." When Micah chuckled, she lowered the mug to the table and gave him a serious look. "I'm not joking. You've always stood out from the others in the pack. At least to me."

"Because you've always had a thing for the bird with the broken wing." He peeled the label from the bottle, suddenly wishing he'd decided to go home once he knew Esme was sleeping. "Or the pup with no parents."

"It was wrong of them to abandon you the way they did, whoever they were."

"I'm lucky Ezra's parents were decent enough to help me out. They were better parents than mine ever were." Even now, all these years later, the thought of them was like a knife to the gut. They'd been ashamed of him. Afraid of what it meant to have him as a son. Unwilling to admit their child was different—through no fault of his own. One morning he'd woken up to find them gone. Dressers empty, closets bare. Car gone. A little money for food, though it didn't help much that he was barely ten years old at the time and wasn't exactly prepared to go grocery shopping.

They'd done him one favor. One single act of mercy.

They hadn't told anybody why they were leaving. Even Ezra's mother might not have been willing to take him in if she'd heard rumors of a witchy wolf pup somewhere in the area. Then again, the Shotgun Falls pack mothers had insisted on Sylvia staying with them after her mate's death. It didn't matter to them that she was a witch.

He'd wandered in the right direction when looking for help. He'd ended up being found by Ezra and Xavier when they were out playing in the woods.

"You're troubled."

He barely stifled a laugh, still half-lost in memory. "No kidding. It's been a troubling couple of days."

"It runs deeper than that. You can't fool me." Folding her arms on top of the table, she leaned in. "You like her. I know you do. You're worried what that means."

Sure. That was also on his mind. If only that was the worst of it.

"For what it's worth, my Kristoff and I were very happy for a long time. It didn't matter to him, my being a witch, any more than it mattered to me that he was a shifter. We were meant for each other. That was all that counted."

"Not everyone is as lucky as you two were."

"Lucky?" A smile floated over her face. "Yes. Not so lucky to lose each other so early, but to have found each other at all."

"If you're trying to talk me into a relationship with Esme, you don't have to go to all the trouble. There's a lot more to it than feelings." There was no way to avoid it. "Will she have to go up in front of the council for what she did?"

"I'm not sure." She sipped her tea, frowning now. "If she does, I know they'll take the past into account. The torment she went through thanks to that cruel Derek. If some of the others who Derek attacked are willing to come forward, that will help. But the council might come down hard on her."

"Will they strip her powers?"

Her forehead creased like she was in pain, and he wished he hadn't asked. "I don't think so. Things aren't the way they used to be. There's a lot more understanding now."

"I hope that's true."

"I'm sure she'll be fine, either way. She'll have a lot of support." They shared a brief smile, and he knew she understood. He wasn't about to abandon Esme now, though he was also no fool. It wouldn't be easy at first. Jordan would be out for blood, or at least vengeance.

A noise from upstairs made them look up. "She shouldn't be awake yet." Sylvia rose, but Micah was faster.

"Let me." He was practically crawling out of his skin, wanting to see her, and his wolf wouldn't be satisfied until he did. There was only so much dissatisfied pacing and snarling and growling he could handle.

By the time he reached the guest bedroom, Esme was sitting up with her feet on the floor. It looked like she was trying to get up but didn't have the strength yet. "Micah." Her voice was weak but clear. "I thought I heard you downstairs. I wanted to—"

"I know what you wanted to do, because you're the most stubborn person I ever met." He didn't have the heart to be annoyed, not really. He would've wanted to see her, too, even if he was laid up. "Come on. Back in bed."

"What is this?" She plucked at the nightgown Sylvia had put on her.

"It's better than a bloodstained sweater, that's what it is." He pulled back the blankets and gently but firmly lowered her to the bed. "And this is a lot more comfortable than a cold, hard rock in the middle of the woods. Your life is improving by the minute."

"But you. You." Once she was down again, her head on the pillow and the blankets drawn over her, she reached up and took his face in her hands. "Are you okay?"

"I'm fine. You know how shifters are. We heal in no time."

She frowned in spite of his attempts at being lighthearted. "You know what I mean."

He leaned down, indulging in a kiss. Still not the ideal spot for this kind of thing, but better than before. At least now they were in bed. Her arms slid around him, and he did the same to her, holding her as tight as he dared. She was still recovering, and not as strong as him even when she was healthy. Something he'd have to keep in mind.

Was he really looking ahead to a future for them? His wolf seemed satisfied with the notion, quieting down, able to rest now.

Half of him hoped she would forget what she was so worried about by the time he sat up to catch his breath, but he knew better than to think she'd let it go. Why would she? She'd seen something unexpected out there.

"Why didn't you tell me?" She stared up at him with those eyes of hers. Eyes that seemed to see everything, to see right through him. "Why didn't you tell me what you can do?"

Even now, with his arms around her and nobody but the two of them in this room, he couldn't bring himself to talk about it. Years of shame, of knowing his parents had abandoned him because of the magic he couldn't control and hadn't asked for. It wasn't the sort of thing a person could forget.

Besides, this wasn't the time for it. "I didn't know

I could do it. That's the truth. We can talk about it later, when you're well again." Though he doubted he'd want to talk about it then, either. He would've rather forgotten all about it. After all, he'd gotten this far in life without using his powers. Why start now?

She didn't like his response, but that came as no surprise. Even now, too weak to get up from the bed, she was determined to have things her way. Her mouth opened, questions written all over her beautiful face.

It was Sylvia who spoke first, her voice floating up the stairs and down the hall. "Micah? There's a call for you down here." There was an edge to her voice, too, telling him the news wasn't great.

He looked down at Esme, letting his fingers trail over her cheek. "It's not over yet, sorry to say. I have to go for now, but—"

She pressed her fingers to his lips, cutting him off. "It's okay. Go on." She even managed a weak smile.

"AND THAT'S IT. That's what happened." Micah sat back in the chair, looking around at his pack. His family. "She managed a spell at the last second, and that's how you found them the way you did. Otherwise, it could've been a very different outcome."

"You took a big gamble, going after her like that." Adam rubbed his scruff-covered jaw, sighing like he was the one who'd trekked across the woods with an injured witch. Like he was exhausted.

"What else was I supposed to do? Let them kill her? I know we're not exactly on the best terms with witches in general, but she did the pack a solid." He glanced toward Ezra.

"She needed the help, and she deserved it." Ezra stepped up beside Micah, a hand on his shoulder.

Adam shrugged with a sigh. "Nobody's arguing that. From what Micah described, I'm surprised nobody cursed them before now. You don't screw with witches unless you want to risk them coming after you."

Logan snickered from his spot in the corner. He tended to hang around on the fringes after years of living outside the pack, but he was trying to be part of things now. Even if that meant hanging around on the edge of situations. "Derek? You think he honestly believed anybody would come after him? He thinks he's untouchable."

No argument there. Micah looked around

Adam's living room, where much of the pack had come together after handing Derek and the others over to their pack—and only after receiving the assurance, they'd be locked down more securely this time around. It looked like everybody was in agreement, that they had his back.

Good thing, too, since a sudden commotion outside the house heralded the arrival of Jordan and a few of his pack. "Here we go." Adam threw his shoulders back before marching out to meet his guests. Micah, Ezra, and the rest followed.

Jordan was predictably beside himself. "You." He thrust a finger in Micah's direction. "The problem I have is with you."

"The problem you have is with your son." Adam folded his arms, standing toe-to-toe with the other alpha. "And his friends. And while we're at it, your security system. Or else they wouldn't have been able to get away like they did."

Jordan's eyes swirled amber, promising a shift. One of the pack members standing near him clamped a hand over his shoulder, muttering something about being careful. It was enough to subdue his wolf, but barely. "Watch what you say."

It wasn't his place, but Micah couldn't hold his tongue. "Considering your son and his friends tried to kill me more than once this morning, you might be the one who should watch what he says. You knew what he was doing all this time, but you did nothing to stop him."

"How dare you?" He made a move like he wanted to lunge, but members of both packs got between them to make sure nothing came of it. Ezra shot Micah a warning look, but he didn't see what Esme went through. He hadn't heard the pain when she recounted that first time. Those three days of hell.

"How dare you? Why don't we start there?" Micah reached into his back pocket and closed his fingers around the bracelet. Now he was doubly glad he'd thought to take it before they left that shack. "Here. This belongs to your son." He tossed it into the air, sunlight glinting off the metal.

Jordan snatched it, held it up to examine. "What's this supposed to be?"

"It's a bracelet, obviously. The bracelet Esme was wearing when I found her in the woods. The same sort of bracelet she wore before. When Derek first did this."

Jordan could try all he wanted to fake ignorance, but it was wasted effort. Guilt touched the corners of his eyes, making them crinkle. Micah jumped on that. "She told you about it, didn't she? And you remember. How could you forget?"

"What about it?" Jordan closed his fist around the links, but his attitude had changed. Some of the arrogance and outrage had drained from him.

Adam snickered. "You must be joking. You know what it means."

"You sheltered him." Micah's wolf growled in his head, anger growing with every breath. "You allowed this to happen. Some might say the curse could've been avoided if you had dealt with your son when this first started. Instead, you dismissed Esme's story." Another growl from his wolf, loud enough that it drowned out the sounds around him. She deserved justice.

"Now we all know." Ezra snarled, looking the alpha up and down. "And we'll be there when he's taken to task this time. We all will."

Adam wasn't quite so cold, but his tone was firm. "You know you're going to have to do something about him. I understand how this complicates things for your pack, but it has to be done."

"What about the curse? When will the curse be lifted?" In the end, he was a concerned father. Micah remembered how he'd leaned over his son, the fear and concern he wasn't able to hide.

Time to take a gamble. "Esme's recovering, but I'm sure she'd be willing to show up when you get your pack together to announce the punishment Derek and the rest of them are going to face now. She can tell you how to lift the curse then."

Ezra disguised a laugh with a cough, but not well enough. Jordan's eyes flashed. "There's nothing amusing about this."

"We know that." Adam didn't look at Ezra, but Micah felt his disapproval in the air. "Especially when one of our own was attacked by six of yours earlier today. This is no laughing matter. What will it be? Where will this event take place?"

Jordan was cornered, and he knew it. Even the tough guys behind him looked like they were deflating, no matter how they bared their teeth and sneered at their rivals. "My compound. Tomorrow, first light." With that he stormed away, the bracelet dangling from his clenched fist.

Adam exhaled, shaking his head as they watched Jordan make his exit. "We'll see what happens now."

14

"I'm telling you, I'm fine. I can handle this."

Sylvia looked skeptical, and Esme could understand why. She was not fine. She wasn't even sure she could handle seeing Derek again, even if he was restrained somehow. He would have to be. They all would.

"I don't see why you have to be there in person. Isn't it enough to send word? I could go for you. I'll tell them what to do."

For one brief, tempting moment, she considered this. The bed was so comfortable, so warm and soft. If Esme didn't know better, she would think her cousin had cast some sort of charm on it.

And she was still so tired. So weak. That wasn't helping.

Her mind wasn't weak, though. "I'll regret it for the rest of my life if I don't see this happen with my own eyes. I have to face him, as much as I don't want to."

Sylvia sighed before patting Esme's cheek. "Fair enough. You just let me know if we need to leave. Squeeze my arm." Esme agreed, but then she would've agreed to just about anything. So long as it meant watching Derek get what he deserved.

If, of course, his father was willing to play along.

It would've been nice if she could've talked to Micah about this, but all he did was leave word with Sylvia about the meeting set up for this morning. She was hoping he would come back after going off to talk to the pack. That maybe they would spend a little time together, that he would hang around while she was resting up. That was selfish, though, and she was being needy. The one thing she didn't want was for him to think she was too needy.

It wasn't like she didn't know how to take care of herself, anyway. She'd been doing it for long enough.

But it was nice, having him around. Being able to lean on him.

"I'm sure he'll be there." There she went,

freaking Esme out the way she sometimes dead. For a witch without her powers, Sylvia had a way of picking up on unspoken feelings. It was eerie.

"Of course he will. He has every right to be. Derek wanted to kill him."

Sylvia only chuckled, opening the passenger side door of her late model car. The sound seemed louder than it should in the middle of a silent, frigid early morning, the rest of the street quiet as a graveyard. "I'm sure that has nothing to do with it."

"You should've been there." Esme lowered herself into the car. "No, on second thought. You shouldn't have. I'm glad you weren't." Sylvia left lightly, closing the door before walking around the front of the car and joining Esme behind the wheel.

"That's not what I mean, and you know it." Though she looked Esme up and down, eyes narrowing. "Or maybe you don't. You were unconscious, after all."

"What do you mean? What did I miss?" And why, oh why, did her heart skip a beat? A brief, intense image flashed across her mind's eye. Micah, kneeling at her bedside, professing his love. Where did that come from? Why in the world would he ever do anything like that?

Kissing in the middle of a life-or-death situation was one thing. They had reached out to each other, found a little comfort. It was necessary, even. Something to keep them both going.

But she wasn't a child. And she wasn't going to talk herself into believing there was more to them than met the eye. Not again, not the way she'd spent almost her entire relationship with Derek convincing herself he was better than he was. That he really loved her, that they would make it as a couple.

Look where it got her. No, Micah wasn't the same sort of man. Not even close. Still, he was a shifter—one with witch's blood in his veins, too. Talk about complicated.

Sylvia's response only complicated things worse than ever. "Let's just say I've known him most of his life, and I've never seen him like that. Beside himself. Frantic. Asking again and again, all the way to my house, if there was anything he could do. Begging me to make you better."

Now she wished she hadn't asked. Now she liked him more than ever, much more than she should have. Now she felt hopeful. Hope was dangerous. "Do you know him well?"

"I wouldn't say that. I've watched him run

around since he was a pup. I know the sort of antics he and his friends got up to when they were growing up. I guess I paid more attention to him because he was virtually an orphan."

"Virtually."

"His parents… They abandoned him when he was very young. I don't know why." Sylvia shook her head, wearing a mournful look as they turned onto the road leading up the mountain, to where Jordan's pack considered their headquarters.

"They were both shifters?"

Sylvia shot her a questioning glance. "Of course."

"I was just wondering." She searched around in her mind for an excuse. "It's just from everything I've learned about shifters, they don't randomly decide to leave one of their own. You're saying they left the entire pack?"

"According to what he said. They emptied the house of everything except him. They didn't leave word of where they were going or if they'd ever return. Then they never did, of course." Sylvia grumbled under her breath. Esme wondered if she was thinking about how much she'd wanted kids with Kristoff, how they were never fortunate enough. It must've made her blood boil, knowing there were parents willing to walk out on their children.

Esme stared out the window, chewing her lip as she mulled this over. There was still an ever-present warmth in her side, but it was nothing like the pain she'd endured in the woods. That burning, agonizing pain, the sense that her muscles were tearing to shreds with every move she made. It made her remember everything Micah had done for her, all the pains he'd taken to make sure she was safe.

He knew what it was like to be alone. No wonder he carried that sense of loneliness and sadness around with him. In a way, they were very much alike. Maybe that was why they were drawn to each other, even when they were fighting. "What did he do?"

"He ended up wandering the woods for a long time until he made it to Shotgun Falls, living most of the time as his wolf. He was taken in by Ezra's family when he and some of the other pups found him. They treated him like one of their own."

"I'm glad he had somebody to take care of him." And she was glad, too, that Micah's useless parents hadn't announced to anybody why they were leaving. It was obvious to her. They must've seen what was different about him. Maybe there was witchcraft somewhere in his bloodline, somehow. Maybe his mother wasn't strictly a one-man sort of woman. Who knew?

At least they had given him a chance by keeping his witch side to themselves. Otherwise, there was no telling what his former pack would've done to him. Poor baby. He must've been so scared, so alone. If he'd been anywhere near her at that moment, she would've thrown her arms around him and cried on his shoulder. She would've promised she would never abandon him the way his parents had.

That wasn't her place, though, was it?

The familiar sight of the compound coming up ahead pushed thoughts of Micah's past to the back of her mind, at least for the time being. Her stomach clenched when memories of that first, terrible meeting came back with a vengeance. Jordan was so cold. Unfeeling. The shock of that had almost been worse than anything else. Realizing he truly didn't care.

There weren't any guards at the gate, which had been left open. Esme soon understood why.

"Well, well, well." Sylvia's headlights swept over the courtyard in front of the mansion, where cars were practically parked one on top of the other. There were more coming up behind, too. "This looks like the place to be this morning, doesn't it? No wonder they're simply letting visitors drive up. It would take all day to question every driver."

"I had no idea it would be like this." And now, Esme regretted dragging herself out of bed more than ever. How was she supposed to speak in front of so many shifters? She didn't recognize any of the men and women still climbing out of their vehicles and filing into the area behind the mansion.

"What's back there?" Sylvia peered into the darkness. The sky was starting to lighten, but the woods behind the mansion were still too dark to see into.

"There's sort of a clubhouse back there, like a big space where Jordan throws fancy parties for his pack. I guess it's the only place on property that can hold all these people." And even then, Esme had to wonder if there'd be enough room.

Everybody wanted to see what would happen. And they would all hate her.

"I don't think this was a good idea." She pressed her hands together, holding them between her knees. "What if they decide to do something to me?"

"You'll stop them before that can happen."

Esme turned to her cousin with her mouth hanging open. "How can you be so confident? I barely have my powers right now. I'm not at full strength."

Sylvia heaved a sigh. "They'd be stupid to attack you, especially with the entire Shotgun Falls pack supporting you."

"You're awfully sure they're supporting me."

"If you'd seen Micah when you were unconscious, believe me. You wouldn't have any doubts."

It might've been rude, but Esme snickered. "No offense, but I'd feel a lot better if I heard that coming from Micah." She blew out a sigh of her own, one tinged with pain. "He never did come back yesterday. He made it sound like he would."

"He had things to do. Besides, he needed rest as much as you did." Sylvia covered her hands with one of her own, squeezing her assurance. "You'll be fine. Everything will be. And you'll finally get to see that nasty piece of work get what's coming to him. Personally, I can hardly wait." She squeezed again, and this time it helped take the edge off Esme's fear.

There was nothing to be afraid of. Micah would be there. He promised nothing would ever happen to her, right? That she'd be safe with his pack. Time to see whether he meant it.

The air was so cold when she got out of the warm car. She pulled the coat's collar tight around her throat, glad Sylvia had gone to the trouble of going to the cabin for some clothes and personal items. Sylvia tucked a hand in her elbow. "Ready?"

"No, but let's go, anyway." They walked slowly, though, thanks to Esme's lingering weakness. She could see more of the huge stone clubhouse with every passing second now that the sun was on its way up. The big windows gave her a look at the number of people inside. Her legs threatened to turn to stone, but she wouldn't let herself give in. Not when she had come this far.

The moment she and Sylvia stepped into the clubhouse, all conversation ended. Silence. Immediate, deafening silence. She resisted the impulse to look at the floor, keeping her head up. Not arrogant, but not afraid, either. She had cursed shifters, sure, but she had her reasons. They would understand once she had a chance to speak up.

At least, she hoped they would. Otherwise, they'd have her guts for garters.

There he was. It only took a few seconds of sweeping the room before she found Micah standing on the opposite side with Ezra, Logan, Drake—she remembered him from Ezra's house. Their eyes met, and Micah flashed a quick smile, nodding a little.

You can do this. She could practically hear him in her head.

One thing was absolutely for sure: it was a good thing her powers were weak, because she couldn't have handled the amount of energy being flung her way otherwise. All the protection spells in the world couldn't have buffered the intense level of resentment, curiosity, anger. Outrage. Sylvia held her arm a little tighter, making a soothing sound in the back of her throat. Like she was comforting a baby.

Adam, the alpha from Micah's pack, met them. "You can come over and stand with us." He said it a little louder than was necessary, probably for the benefit of everybody standing nearby. He wanted to make it clear she had his support, even if there was obvious, gritty tension behind his invitation. So he wasn't exactly a fan of hers, but a promise was a promise. How much convincing had Micah needed to do? How many favors did he owe? She sneaked another look at him, but he was talking with a couple of his friends.

They had arrived just in time, since the double doors at the far end of the structure opened, and Jordan Greystone marched in. Was his black hair starting to go white? She wondered if her curse had anything to do with that. Behind him was a dozen shifters, some of whom she recognized from her time with Derek.

And there was Derek himself, along with the others she'd cursed. They looked like death—drawn, pale, shaky, sweaty. They were sick. She had done that to them.

She wouldn't have if they hadn't already been sick, deep down inside.

Jordan fixed his gaze on her, pinning her in place when he came to a stop in the center of the room. The air was thick, almost too thick to breathe. "I trust you plan to lift this curse today." Even now, he was haughty. Full of his own importance. When would he learn?

She lifted her chin, meeting him head-on. "I already explained to Derek how the curse works. He has to be the one to lift it." A chorus of disbelieving mutters rose up. Only the Shotgun Falls shifters stayed silent.

"How would a shifter lift a curse, unless he had witch's blood?" Now there was snickering, even soft laughter. Esme cringed inside but fought with all her might not to look at Micah. Not to give him away.

"All he has to do is admit what he did. No sorcery involved." She found Derek's furtive glare and met it with her own hard, cold stare. "That's it. You can end this right now. All you have to do is take responsibility."

Derek looked at his father. "This is ridiculous. You know she's lying."

Jordan turned to him. "Do I?" He stuck a finger in the pocket of his slacks and pulled out a familiar bracelet. Esme gasped softly at the sight. "What about this? Where did this come from? You swore you cut ties with that dark coven in Denver, yet here we are. I can all but taste the magic coming from this simple chain. Speak up. Admit what you've done."

He was trapped, and he knew it. Esme couldn't help but take a little pleasure in watching him squirm. All eyes were on him. They knew, they all did. Word tended to spread. None of them had done anything to stop it, though, had they? Let them stare and mutter and shake their heads all they wanted.

"Do it." One of Derek's cursed friends held his head in his hands. "If it'll lift the curse, do it."

"Fine." Derek threw his head back, sweaty hair flopping back from his forehead when he did. "Yeah. I went to the coven. They provide what I ask for."

"What did you do?" Jordan was stiff, frozen in place, staring at his son.

Derek lifted his broad shoulders. "We used them on witches. We'd make them powerless, then chase them through the woods. It was just a game." Micah growled loud enough for Derek to hear. Derek glanced his way before looking at the floor.

"From what I heard, it wasn't a game." Jordan stepped up closer, towering over his now shrinking, slumped son. "You terrorized defenseless creatures. Repeatedly. Deliberately. I didn't want to believe it."

"We were only having fun."

"Fun?" Jordan took Derek by the shoulders. "Fun for whom?" He shook him hard enough that Derek's head flopped back and forth.

"So you admit it?" That was Adam, raising his voice above the noise coming from all around them. "You admit what you've all done?"

"We did it." Derek's friends nodded firmly, miserably. "We did." Derek nodded, too.

Esme felt it before they did. The curse lifting, the energy dissipating like smoke on the wind. One of the afflicted shifters sank to his knees, almost weeping. "Thank you, thank you." He fell onto his side, eyes closed. One of his buddies joined him, kneeling with his hands over his face.

Derek blinked hard, shaking his head like he was clearing the cobwebs. "It worked. I feel it."

Jordan didn't return his bright, relieved smile. He took a step back, looking at Adam before turning to other packs and their alphas. There was no question of what had to be done now. Even Esme knew it. There had to be payment for his crimes. His so-called fun. "There's nothing I can do for you now. The council will decide what happens next."

Derek's head snapped up, eyes bulging. Like he didn't believe his father would do this. "But—but wait—" It was too late. A group of tall, hulking shifters—big even for their species—came in and took him and his friends away. They tried to argue, begged for forgiveness, but it was too late for them.

"What will happen now?" Esme didn't ask the question of anyone in particular as she watched Derek being dragged off.

"The council will want to lock them up for a while." Ezra patted her shoulder, sort of awkwardly. "You won't have to worry about them anymore." They watched as Jordan walked out, his body rigid. What would it mean for his pack, losing the alpha's son? The heir apparent?

It wasn't her problem. She told herself to be glad he got what was coming to him. This was what she wanted.

Only she wanted something more now. She wanted someone more.

Someone who was already gone. She looked around, hoping, but Micah was nowhere in sight.

Sylvia tugged her arm. "Come on. Let's get you back in bed before you fall over." Esme tried to ignore the sympathy in her voice. Like she understood but was too kind to say anything.

15

"I knew I'd find you here."

Micah jumped at the sound of Ezra's voice, coming from behind him. He'd been too busy swimming in the past to hear his friend's approach. He hadn't even sensed the presence of another shifter. He was that out of it.

He stood and brushed leaves from his jeans. "I was thinking about going on a long run. Another minute and I might've been gone."

"Good thing I followed you." Ezra stood next to him, shoulder to shoulder, both of them looking out over the valley. Over Shotgun Falls.

"The humans down there don't have the first idea what happened today." Micah glanced at his friend, his brother. "Doesn't that blow your mind?"

"It does. Like living in two separate worlds. They have no idea how close they came to witnessing a full-on war between us and the witches."

"Neither of whom they know exists."

"Exactly."

Micah felt Ezra's attentive gaze. So did his wolf, who stood at attention, waiting to see what would happen now. There had to be a reason why Ezra had sought him out after the gathering at Jordan's compound. Finally, he got tired of waiting. "What made you look for me here?"

"It's where we found you. Xavier and me." Ezra heaved a sigh, thrusting his hands into the pockets of his puffy vest. "Even back then, I remember thinking it must've taken you ages to come all this way. You must've gone through hell."

"It wasn't that bad." Really, most of it was too dim and blurry to qualify as memory. "I try not to think about it."

"Understandable." Ezra nudged him. "You like her. A lot. I know you do."

"How do you know that?"

"For starters, you practically ran away from her the second things wrapped up back there. You ran away from all of us. Don't pretend you didn't. We're past that point, you know?"

"What does it matter? We both know it won't fly. A shifter and a witch."

"Kristoff and Sylvia—"

"Kristoff and Sylvia are one single example of that kind of mating working out, and you know it." Micah shot a look at his friend. "And she ended up with her powers stripped because of it, in case you forgot. I don't want that for Esme."

"Is that what you're worried about? Times are different now."

"Are they? Have things changed that much?" Micah groaned, scrubbing his hands over his head, his face. He'd hardly gotten any sleep despite his best efforts. Much more of this, and he'd be running on fumes. "Because last I checked, an untold number of witches were terrorized for no reason, and nobody did anything about it. We don't mix in their world, and they don't mix in ours, right? Very convenient."

"It doesn't have to be that way."

"You're right. It doesn't. But that's how it is right now, and right now's what matters."

"If you think any of us would care about you mating with a witch, you're wrong. Besides, you're the one who always seemed to have a problem with witches. Not us." Ezra snorted, dangerously close to a laugh. "It's okay to admit you were wrong about them, you know. Nobody's going to hold it against you."

"What if I told you..." Micah turned his back to Ezra, unable to look him in the eye now. He never planned on telling anybody, not even his closest friend. "I figured this was something I could hide indefinitely. That it didn't have to matter."

"What? About having a thing for a witch?"

"No. That's not what I mean."

"What do you mean, then? Out with it. You're not usually cryptic like this." Ezra shoved him from behind. "Come on."

"It won't make a difference? No matter what I tell you?"

"Hey." No more shoving this time. No more playing. Ezra took him by the shoulder and turned him around until they were face-to-face. "You know me better than that. Or I thought you did."

"Some things transcend a long friendship, even one as close as ours." When Ezra only stared in response, Micah sighed. He'd come too far to back off now. "Somehow, for some reason, I have witch's blood. That's why my parents left. They couldn't handle the shame."

Ezra's face fell. "Witch blood? How?"

"Your guess is as good as mine. I was maybe eight or nine when it started showing itself." It was never easy, dredging up the past, but it had to be done. "Mom would lose something, and I'd know where it was without looking. Dad would break the lawnmower, and I'd know how to fix it. I was just a kid, but I... I knew. I knew who was calling on the phone before they picked up. And once I woke up and announced Mom's sister was badly injured during a hunt. They got word of it an hour later."

"Wow. I guess they didn't react well."

"They walked out on me. I'd say you're right." He chuckled, bitter. "That didn't happen until Mom knocked a vase off the kitchen table. I caught it without using my hands. I don't know how to this day, I really don't. I... thought about stopping it, keeping it from hitting the floor. And I did. It hovered, then landed gently, right side up."

He sighed at the memory. "I'll never forget the look on her face. Not relief, not even surprise. It was disgust."

"I'm really sorry. That had to be tough." Ezra's expression revealed sympathy, pain, concern. Miles away from the disgust Micah was expecting. "No wonder you always felt like you did about witches, huh?"

"It's the reason I ended up alone."

"But you're not alone. That didn't last. I found you out here that day, and you've been part of our pack ever since."

"And now?" He couldn't help but feel skeptical. "Am I part of the pack now?"

Ezra's head snapped back. "Why wouldn't you be?"

"For starters, what I just told you."

Ezra was too much of a straight shooter to pretend he didn't understand. He ran a hand over the back of his neck, cheeks puffing out when he sighed. "Listen. I'm not going to pretend it doesn't matter, you having mixed blood. But it doesn't matter as much as you think it does. You're a wolf. You're part of us."

He lowered his brow. "But you're part of them, too. And you shouldn't have to turn your back on either one in favor of the other."

"That's all fine and good to say, but is it true? That's what I want to know."

"It's true if you decide it is. You're in charge of your destiny, man." Ezra laughed at himself. "I sound like a self-help guru or whatever, but I mean it. I'd back you. I know Adam and Logan and Drake and everybody else would, too."

"I appreciate that. I know it doesn't sound that way, but I do." He shrugged. Guilt ate at him. "I don't know who I want to be, though. I know you'd have my back. I just don't know if I want to have anything to do with that side of me."

He looked down at his hands, flexing his fingers. "I did something to them. Derek, those guys. I didn't mean to. It happened."

"What happened?"

He thought back. It didn't take much concentrating to remember the moment clearly. "Esme was in trouble. They were closing in around her. Derek was about to hurt her, maybe kill her. And this... this force rose up in me. Like when the wolf is about to take over, and you feel that surge of power." He cast a questioning look to Ezra, who nodded his understanding.

"And then, all of a sudden, a ball of light shot out from my hands and hit them. It was enough to knock them back so I could get to her."

"Just like the wolf can take over a young shifter before they know how to control it. When emotions run high, I mean. Remember those days?"

Did he ever. It wasn't enough for hormones to make him walk around with a tent pitched in front of him half the time. He'd also had to wrestle his wolf into submission more times than he could count.

"But you learned, right?" Ezra was wearing one of his know-it-all looks. "We all learned. You could learn to control your witch side, too. Otherwise, who knows? You could end up frying somebody for cutting you off in traffic."

"I never thought about it that way."

"No kidding." Ezra grinned, going a long way toward convincing Micah he was sincere. That, plus the sense of peace from his wolf, left him feeling sure of himself for the first time in days. No, in his entire life. It had always been there, that fear. Would somebody see it in him? Smell it on him? The thing that made him different, the thing that made his own parents turn their backs on him?

Ezra's grin slipped. "Does she know?"

No need to ask who he meant. "Yeah. She saw it. She's got a million questions, I guess."

"You guess? You don't know?"

"Don't start with me." Micah held his hands up, palms out, and was shocked when Ezra threw an arm over his face.

"Careful. Those hands are dangerous." Ezra lowered his arm, snickering. "Sorry. I couldn't help it."

Micah rolled his eyes as he started back for his car, left in the clearing nearby. "I'm supposed to be the one with the quips and remarks, remember? You're the broody one, I'm the smartass. Don't steal my shtick."

They walked in silence for a little while, which Micah appreciated. He needed to get his thoughts together. Something still bugged him, left him feeling apprehensive. Finally, he had to say it. "They wanted to flay her alive today. Some of the members from the other packs. Denver, Pueblo."

"No kidding."

"Let's not pretend it'd be easy. Announcing we were mates, I mean. She hasn't made many friends, acting like she did."

"But." Ezra held up a finger. "They heard what Derek and those idiot friends of his did. They know she wasn't cursing them for some petty reason. They deserved worse than what she gave them, if you ask me."

"Much worse." He could still hear them taunting her. Screaming, laughing, howling. Derek's shouts echoed in his memory. *You're dead.* There was still not a shred of doubt in his mind that Derek had meant it.

"But come on." Micah rolled his eyes. "You think that'll be enough to wipe out the bad blood?"

"That, and time. It'll take time."

Time. That was something he had, or thought he did. What he didn't possess was patience.

And Ezra knew it. "You don't have to wait that long. You can decide for yourself to get rid of your stupid prejudices and go after what you want. You'll have our support, all the way."

"That's easy for you to say, standing where you are."

They came to a stop at Micah's truck. Ezra turned to him, and he wasn't grinning. Not a trace of humor. "Listen to me. When I was cursed, I was afraid to tell you or anybody. I spiraled. I was sure all of you would reject me because my wolf had."

"We wouldn't have."

"Yeah, well, I couldn't imagine that at the time." He jerked his chin at Micah. "So, what makes you so different?"

"Starting with my mixed blood?"

"You didn't ask to have it. No more than I asked to be cursed. And you can't do anything about it now besides trying to hide it, which could end up making life a lot worse if you end up losing control one day. You need to learn how to control it."

"You're right."

Now Ezra grinned. "And what do you know? You have a witch in your life who can teach you."

"If she wants to. We're standing around making things up in our heads for all I know." What a miserable feeling. Wanting somebody with all of him, with everything he possessed, and not knowing whether she felt the same way. "Was it like this for you? With Hope?"

"You mean the incredible, heart-stopping uncertainty? Being sure you don't know what you're doing from one minute to the next? Feeling like everything you say and do is wrong, and you're only going to screw the entire thing up?"

"Something like that."

Ezra's face went stony. "No. I have no idea what that's like." He couldn't keep a straight face until he was finished, cracking a grin halfway through. "But you get through it, because the result is worth the hassle. At least, that's how I see Hope."

And it was without a doubt how Micah saw Esme. She was worth the hassle.

The only question now, did she feel the same about him?

16

"I told you. I don't want to hang out with those girls. Hope and the rest of them." Esme chewed her lip, staring out through the window over the kitchen sink. "But thank you for the invite."

"This has nothing to do with them." Sylvia's laughter was soft, musical. "It has to do with you, and with the way you've retreated back to your cave. I thought you'd be glad now that he's locked away where he belongs. You're free, and I refuse to speak his name."

Free. That was a funny word. "Terrific. I'm free to get dirty looks, and nasty comments muttered behind my back. Every shifter in Colorado has a problem with me now."

"I doubt that, dear."

Easy for her to say. She didn't have to go through life with a target on her back. "Trust me. It's better for me to lay low."

"But it's been over a week now. Surely everyone's put this behind them."

To think, the woman had lived among shifters all these years, but understood so little about them. Only what she wanted to understand.

No. That was unfair. One thing Esme tried never to do was be dishonest with herself. Even with the curse, she hadn't kidded herself. She'd known there might be consequences. Now, she reminded herself of what her cousin had gone through. Powers stripped, banished from the coven.

The pack took her in after Kristoff's death when they could've just as easily thrown her own the way the coven did. Was it any surprise she felt so warmly toward them? So fond of them?

"Either way, I'm not looking forward to finding out." She looked over her shoulder, toward the stove, and twirled her pointer finger in the air. One of the knobs turned, lighting the jet under the kettle. Sure, she could've gone about it the normal, human way, but now that her powers were fully back she wanted to take advantage of them.

And test them. That was never far from the back of her mind. Sometimes she woke up from a dead sleep, sure she was powerless. That the goddess had changed her mind and taken away the magic.

The one person she wanted to share this with had vanished. That was the worst part. Whenever she'd wake up with her heart in her throat and a chill running down her spine, Esme wanted to turn to Micah and tell him everything. She wanted to curl up in his arms and let him comfort her. Nothing ever seemed quite so bad when she was with him.

He wanted nothing to do with her. She'd known it, felt it. Otherwise, why had he disappeared? Were things with his pack really that complicated now?

No, their... thing, whatever it was, had been situational. She had known it, had tried to guard herself against catching feelings for him. He was a protective person by nature. Anything he'd felt for her came from that, from feeling like her life was his responsibility.

Now? No such responsibility. No feelings. He probably never thought about her, while he was the only thing Esme could think about.

There she went, letting a man get to her again. Letting him ruin her life—even if this time, he'd also saved it.

"Stop by the store. Please. There's something I want to show you."

Esme lifted a brow, looking over the row of potted plants on the windowsill. "A new book? Herbology?"

"Something that made me immediately think of you. How's that sound?"

"It sounds like you're bending over backwards to get me to come out to the store."

Sylvia chuckled. "Please, I'm an old woman. Spare my back the effort and come. You won't regret it."

Somehow, Esme doubted it.

"You're here!" Sylvia practically floated across the store when Esme walked in, looking over her shoulder when she did. There were two female shifters out there—no missing the energy any more than she could miss the energy of their distrust. At least it wasn't hatred, though it felt close enough.

"I'm here." Esme wished her cousin would pipe down a little, too, since they were attracting attention. Humans craned their necks to see who deserved this sort of greeting. *Sorry to disappoint you*

—*just a disgraced witch*. She ducked her head, more than a little embarrassed.

"I'm so glad. You look so much better, too." The silver bangles on Sylvia's wrists danced musically when she raised her arms for a hug. It was a comfort, sure, but it didn't answer any questions. Why did she have to be there?

Especially when the shotgun Falls pack mothers were clustered together in their customary spot near the beverage station?

Esme's insides went cold. She added an extra layer to the protection spells surrounding her. "Is this why you wanted me to come in? So I could talk with them?" She nodded slightly in the direction of the group.

"No, no." Sylvia shook her head, beaming for some mysterious reason. "No, it has nothing to do with them. When did you become so suspicious?"

"You know when."

"Well, those days are over. I'll remind you of that as many times as necessary until you believe it." Sylvia took her by the arm, chuckling. "Though if you wouldn't mind, I'd appreciate it not taking too much longer. Come on. I have something to show you."

Instead of leading her deeper into the store,

however, or up the stairs to the second level, Sylvia led her to the door she'd just come through. "Wait. Where are we going?"

"Next door. You'll love it."

"Love what?" Sylvia only shushed her, sweeping outside into the cold and trotting next door. Esme gave up trying to find out what this was about. Better to let Sylvia have her way. Easier, too.

What wasn't easy was pretending to understand why they'd entered an empty store. Not empty of customers. Empty, period. Bare shelves, bare tables, a blank chalkboard hanging above the front counter. "What's going on? Did they close?" It had been a bakery, if memory served. There was still the faint scent of yeasty bread hanging in the air.

"Yes, they closed up shop a couple of weeks ago. I was sorry to see them go." Sylvia released her arm, stepping into the center of the space and taking a deep breath. "I did love their cupcakes."

"So..." Esme looked around. "Why are we here?"

"I wanted to show you the place." Sylvia's lips twitched. "And offer it to you, if you want."

Esme's eyes bulged. Her feet grew roots, holding her in place. "What?" It was all she could manage now that her lungs couldn't see to pull in enough air.

"It's yours, if you want it. To lease, that is."

"Wh-who says?"

"I say." When Esme merely gaped at her, Sylvia responded with a Cheshire Cat smile. "Didn't you know I own this building?"

"Uh, no. That's news to me."

"Sure. I bought both of them when I was setting up shop." Sylvia wandered behind the counter, looking around at the empty shelves behind it. "My original notion was to tear down the wall separating them and use it as one massive bookstore. Before long, I saw the light. Why not rent it out to another entrepreneur and collect the monthly revenue? In the end, it seemed like a smarter move."

"Of course." She didn't mean it, really. She couldn't agree because none of this made sense. Sylvia was two or even three steps ahead of her.

"Now, it's empty. And it's yours if you want it." Sylvia faced her, no longer smiling. "It's strictly a business arrangement, you understand. I'll expect rent on time and for you to take care of the place."

"Hold on a second." It was all so ludicrous, she had to laugh. "I never said I wanted it. I wouldn't even know what to do with it."

"Yes, you would. Stop selling yourself short. Remember what we talked about?"

Sure, she did. She thought about it a lot, more

than she wanted to admit. "But this is so much work."

"Esme. You're..." Sylvia cupped her hands around her mouth, her voice dropping to a stage whisper. "A witch."

"No kidding."

"You can make it easy on yourself. I'm not saying there's any call to bewitch your patrons, but..." She wiggled her fingers in the air with a mischievous grin. "You could enchant the store. People will come in without knowing why they want to. And once they're inside, they'll have your potions and tonics and, I don't know, smudge sticks to choose from."

Enchanting the store. Making things a little easier. Having fun with it. "Hand-poured ritual candles. Classes on how to grow herbs and use them in tonics."

Sylvia laughed. "No, you haven't given this any thought at all."

Esme rolled her eyes. "Okay, the idea intrigued me. That doesn't mean I want to go through with it."

"Yes. You do." No more joking around. Sylvia was as much like a stern parent as Esme had ever seen her, right down to the way she plopped her hands on her hips. "Stop kidding yourself. I don't have my powers anymore, and I can feel how excited you are by this idea. It's a good one. You'd make a fortune. You'd be a blessing to so many people who don't even know yet that they need you."

"No wonder you opened a store. You're a born saleswoman."

"I've had a lot of practice over the years." Sylvia stepped out from behind the counter, shrugging. "It's yours, dear. And I would be right next door if you ever needed me. And if you're interested in hiring help, I know of at least two human girls who'd love to help you out."

Charlotte and Hope. That had to be who she meant. Esme liked them, they got along, but still. "Let's not get too far ahead of ourselves. I haven't even signed the lease yet."

Sylvia wore the look of a triumphant warrior. "Funny you should mention that. I just so happen to have a lease in my office."

Why didn't that come as a surprise?

17

After a lot of talking and brainstorming—and signing—Esme made the drive home from town. It was coming up on dusk, and she wondered if she should've picked up something to eat before heading back. She'd been too busy thinking, planning. Dreaming.

When was the last time she'd let herself dream? To really, truly let go and allow her mind to wander? To envision all the things her life could be? Years. Before Derek came into her life, for sure. Now he was in the past, locked up where he couldn't hurt her or anybody.

And Sylvia had a point. She had to start living sometime. And she was tired of being alone. Her time with Micah had taught her that, if nothing else. It was time to start letting people in her life again.

What a shame he didn't want to be one of those people.

She was just thinking that when she pulled up at the cabin, now enshrouded in darkness.

Only it wasn't dark inside. The kitchen light was on. She hadn't turned it on before leaving. It was still early afternoon then, she had no reason to.

And the door was partly open.

It wasn't fear that held her in place, hands gripping the wheel as she sat and stared at the cabin. Her home, her sanctuary. A sanctuary somebody felt entitled to break into whenever he felt like it. The nerve of him. She wasn't even happy he'd finally decided to show his face.

Because it was him. Micah. She felt it, didn't question it. "The nerve." She flung the car door open and slammed it shut a moment later before marching straight to the half-open door.

Throwing it open, she greeted him with a snarl. "Were you raised in a barn or something? Why do you keep leaving my door hanging open?"

He was bent in front of the open refrigerator, and oh, sweet goddess, had he always looked this good? Flannel button-down, sleeves rolled up to show off his thick forearms. Jeans that set his impressive backside off to perfection. He looked up at her, and a hank of golden hair flopped over his forehead. "Hello to you, too."

"Nope. You don't get to do that." She peeled off her coat and hung it next to the door, where Micah had already hung his. Making himself right at home, wasn't he? "You don't get to show up at my house and pretend like you belong here. Not when you dropped off the face of the earth for the past week. I had no idea where you were or if I'd ever see you again. So please, don't pretend to be offended when I don't greet you with a huge hug and, I don't know, tears or whatever."

He straightened up and closed the fridge, eyes never leaving hers. Eyes she had once watched swirling with both shifter and witch magic. "Are you finished?"

"Shut up. And while you're at it, get out of here. I didn't ask you to come here, and I certainly didn't—"

He was so fast. The shifter part of him at work. One second, he stood across the room. The next he was there, in front of her, holding her, cutting her off with a hard, deep kiss that just about turned her legs to jelly. Not that she needed legs with Micah keeping her upright.

Part of her—a very small, quiet part—wanted to stop him. To push him away and tell him it wouldn't be this easy. He couldn't waltz in and out of her life, then come back and kiss her and expect things to be better. How was she supposed to do that when he wouldn't let her up for air? When his hands slid up and down her back, and his tongue stroked against hers in the most seductive, necessary way?

She'd have to be strong. Time to set some boundaries.

He didn't just let her go. He hit the wall behind him, knocking two framed photos to the floor and probably leaving a dent. "What was that?

"A repelling charm." She straightened her clothes before running an arm over her tingling mouth. "We have a few things to discuss before you start getting all handsy with me." And mouthy. And tonguey.

"I had to find a way to get you to stop yelling at me."

"Bravo." She rolled her eyes and wished her body didn't insist on responding as violently as it did whenever he was involved. She'd practically been at death's door out in the woods, freezing to death on top of that, yet he'd found a way to make her pant for him.

Before she could say anything else, he broke in. "Listen to me, please, before you go off again. I'm sorry I didn't come to see you before now. I'd had things to settle with the pack. I didn't feel comfortable telling you about them until the plans were final."

Plans. The word didn't inspire confidence. "What kind of plans?"

"Plans for my future—or, rather, what I hope my future will be. I guess it's no secret that I'm part-witch."

That blue ball of light filled her memory. The swirling light in his eyes. "No. It's not a secret."

"Until now, I tried to ignore that part of myself. I figured, if I didn't pay attention to it... well, you know."

"Sounds a lot like trying to ignore an amputation."

"Something like that." For a moment, he looked very tired, but also extremely relieved. Like it felt good to speak openly about it. She guessed it had to. "Until recently, I never imagined admitting the truth. I certainly had no plans to develop my powers or learn to harness them."

Her teeth sank into her lip as the meaning behind his words revealed itself. Was he saying what it very much sounded like he was saying? Was she hearing what she wanted to hear?

"Until you." He gave her a helpless little shrug, one that almost struck her as apologetic. "All these years, I held my parents' abandonment against witches in general. It was my witch blood that made them reject me. Now I know, of course, it was their prejudice. I came close to letting their prejudice permanently become mine."

"I'm glad you managed to avoid that."

"Me, too." Though he grimaced like he was unhappy. She realized he was trying to reach for her. Thanks to her charm, there was no hope of it. Leave it to him to keep trying, though. "I want to learn. I want to explore all there is to know. I finally feel whole for the first time in my life. No more hiding who I am."

His sincerity was enough to choke her up. "I'm so glad for you. I really am."

"And I want you to teach me. You've already taught me so much."

"Micah, I'm not—" She tilted her head to the side, squinting. "I did? What did I teach you?"

"For starters, that there's nothing wrong with being a witch. I know it sounds pathetic, but it's true. You taught me about what's important. Whether I want to stand on the sidelines and shake my head and pretend there's nothing I can do, or step up for what's right. I always thought I was the latter, but you showed me otherwise. I could've spoken up to Jordan when I first heard the rumors. I didn't."

"It wouldn't have mattered. He didn't listen to me, remember?"

"I would've been in a better position than you. Shifter, remember?"

Right, and Jordan hated witches. She'd never stood a chance. "Got it."

"I want to be that man. The sort of man you deserve to have by your side. If you'll let me." He grimaced again, tendons standing out on his thick neck as he strained. "Can you lift this spell?"

"Not yet." She folded her arms, tapping a fingertip to her chin. "What about your pack?"

"That's what I was working out. I'm not leaving them. I couldn't. But they understand I'll need a little time away. I'll join them on the full moon hunts, but otherwise I'm going to do my own thing for a while." He snickered. "Though I doubt Ezra would leave me alone for long."

"I wouldn't want him to. I know how much he means to you."

"And that's why I love you."

He looked just as surprised as she was, and he was the one who said it. "You what?"

He gulped. "I love you. I think I've loved you since we first met. You drew me in. I couldn't help but pick little arguments just to have an excuse to talk to you. And now, after everything we went through?" His head swung back and forth. "I can't spend another minute of my life without you in it. You're too precious. I need you too much."

It was almost too much to believe. He loved her. She believed him, felt every ounce of his love filling the room, wrapping itself around her like the warmest, softest blanket. No matter where she went from that moment on, she'd have a blanket of love around her. There was no magic better than that.

She waved her fingers. "You can move now. And I'd like it very much if you kissed me again. Right now."

He crossed the room in two long strides before lifting her in his arms, holding her with her feet dangling above the floor. "So is that a yes? You'll teach me? And, you know. The other thing?"

"What do you think?" She wound her arms around his neck. "It takes two to tango, right? I wouldn't have drawn you to me if we weren't meant for each other. That's how it is with shifters and witches, both. When it's meant to be, there's not much on earth powerful enough to stop it."

She touched her forehead to his before letting out a deep breath. "I do love you. So much." There were tears on her cheeks when he kissed her again and again. Tears of gratitude. Of wonder. Of deep, deep joy.

Joy turned to something else. Something hotter, something located way down in her core. Micah growled softly, pulling back just far enough to look at her. "If you wouldn't mind, there's something I've been wanting to do with you for a while now, and right through that door is the perfect place to do it." He was looking toward the bedroom.

His face fell when she frowned. "Sorry. If that's too much, too fast—"

She silenced him with another kiss. "No. It's just that I was wondering why the kitchen table isn't good enough."

His eyes lit up. "You might be the perfect woman." He carried her to the table and set her on top. Now there was no stopping him, and it was the last thing she wanted, anyway. No more having to hold back because she was sick or in pain or too weak. She indulged in kiss after kiss, each one hotter than the last, while Micah took a tour of her body with both hands.

"You have no idea how much I wanted to do this." There was a wolf's growl under his words, something dangerous. Something primal. Goose-bumps raced over Esme's skin, worse when Micah's mouth traveled over the curve of her jaw. The pressure from his lips sent shockwaves of pure pleasure racing through her veins.

"I think I do." She wrapped her legs around his hips and hauled him in closer, rocking her hips against him until he groaned. It was a beautiful sound, one that made her feel a power unrelated to witchcraft. The power to bring this mountain of a man to his knees.

He lowered her until she was on her back, his hands working her sweater up over her head. Every touch of his skin to hers was like fire, but the sweetest fire she'd ever felt. A fire that blazed brighter with every stroke, every caress.

He brushed a palm over her breast, her nipple pebbling under his touch even through the lacy cup of her bra. He lowered it before running his tongue in a slow circle around the peak. "You're so sweet." She responded with a sigh, arching her back, her body taking over. Taking what it needed.

Just the way her hands did, running through Micah's hair before sliding over his shoulders and back. A hunger swelled up in her, a need to touch more. To feel touch his skin and feel the muscles working under it. When she pulled at his shirt, he tore it over his head and threw it aside with a frustrated grunt. Like even that took too long.

This wasn't the first time she'd ever seen him shirtless, but now there was no need to avert her eyes. Instead, she feasted on the sight of him, tested the firmness of his biceps and the ripples of his abs. They tightened when she crept lower, dipping inside the waistband of his jeans. A long growl rumbled in his chest, and she wondered who was more in control, wolf or man.

Which did she want it to be?

He rolled his hips, grinding against her, and desire wiped away all questions. Desire and heat—driving heat, explosive. The sort of heat that left her fumbling with his belt, desperate to get rid of every stitch of clothing between them. It had never been like this before, like she'd die if she wasn't with him. Really, fully with him. Connected. Mated.

A look into his eyes told her she wasn't alone. They took on an amber light, glowing and warm. It pulled her in, that light. Promised forever. How did she ever believe she could ignore what was between them? She grabbed him by the back of his neck and pulled him down for a deep, scorching kiss. There was no way to be close enough to him.

Though he tried, wedging himself between her thighs before tearing at her panties, growling as he reduced them to shreds. She gasped in surprise, then again when Micah pushed inside her slick tunnel with one smooth, sure thrust.

"Sorry..." He barely sounded like himself, his voice rasping and strained. "Can't... stop..." His breathing deepened, turned into something more like panting. He was as helpless against this as she was.

She responded by linking her legs behind his back, pulling him deeper. A brief smile flashed across his face before he pulled back and drove himself into her again. "Mine."

"Yes." She closed her eyes. "Yes, yes." It was an answer. A plea for more. His body crashed against hers, and she whimpered in approval, jerking upward to meet his thrusts with hers. Working toward climax. Fighting for it.

While Micah fought for his. He pinned her in place, his arms around her, driving himself harder and deeper the way the wolf wanted it. The way she did, too. She cried out her pleasure, her nails raking down his back as the tension built and built in her core. She was about to lose it. She was about to—

"Yes!" She arched again, her nipples brushing his and sending delicious shocks all through her, heightening the intensity of the explosion in her core. "Oh, yes! Micah..." She broke off with a shudder, swept away.

The tea kettle whistled though the stove was off. The very cabin seemed to groan and creek. The overhead lamp flickered, then glowed twice as bright. Esme turned her face away from the blinding light a second before the bulb burned out and plunged them into darkness.

That had never happened before. Any of it. She was almost surprised enough to miss how Micah's rhythm changed, sliding away until he lost control. All she could do was hold on, riding out the wolf's frantic finish. Completing their mating. Making them one.

Micah raised his head long enough to let out a single howl, loud enough to set her hair on end, before he plunged down again and bit into the soft spot between her neck and her shoulder. She arched against him, crying it in surprise and sudden, explosive pleasure. It should've hurt, his bite. It shouldn't have sent her rocketing up and over the edge all over again. Shouldn't have spread waves of sweet warmth washing over her.

Because it's right. Because he's mine, and I'm his. She had never been so sure of anything, and that certainty made her smile. She was still smiling when Micah raised his head to look down at her, wearing a lazy smile of his own. "Wow. That was…"

"Yes." She nodded slowly, gravely. "It was. I'd better start stockpiling lightbulbs."

"Are you kidding?" He planted a kiss on the tip of her nose. "By the time I'm finished with you, you'll need a new house."

All things considered, that didn't sound half bad.

KEEP READING for an excerpt from another Ava Benton book!

EXCERPT: ARKON

Demons aren't real. Are they?

One sexy demon. One human female. One lethal magic dagger.

She's broken. He's on a mission. How did her brokenness derail his mission? Join this sexy demon and the woman who can't deny the attraction to him on a journey for healing, revenge, and sexy times.

Jasmine's life flipped upside down a little more than a decade ago since the fateful day she intervened in a scuffle between two men with horns. Horns! Since that day her family's thought she's bonkers. In more institutions than she cares to remember, on more prescriptions than a junkie, she's finally settled into a semblance of normal in the middle of nowhere, running an antique store. Normal. Totally. Until...

Azar's been haunted by the memory of the girl who saved his life ages ago, but he's had more important things on his mind. Staying alive. He and his brothers are being persecuted by bounty hunters sent by the princes of hell. He's doing everything he can not to be killed. While at the same time, trying to find a way through the veil so he can avenge his parents' murders. Until...

CHAPTER 1

JASMINE

The white and porcelain-blue vase needed to be wiped down. A single crack ran down the side, cutting through the patterned roses and ivy covering the wide base. It wasn't a bad find, considering half the junk that came from my latest haul from the estate sale at the old mansion on the bluff.

"Let's get you cleaned up and put on a shelf," I told the vase, tapping my neon-blue fingernails against it. "You'd look good in the display window, too. I think I have some flowers lying around somewhere."

"Talking to the merchandise again?"

I shrugged when Cara Night, my only employee and one of my only friends, came around the counter carrying another dust-covered crate. "I like to know what's in my shop. I don't think that's a bad thing. Each piece has a story."

She blew a curl of black hair out of her face. Her grin made her hazel eyes crinkle. "Whatever you say, sunshine. I love you, crazy or not."

"Someone has to," I replied with a smirk. I jotted down a note about the vase, then set it and the vase aside on the counter. The surface was already lined with four antique wooden boxes, two more vases, a set of tarnished candlesticks, and an incredibly unique statue of a satyr perched on a tree stump sporting a rather sizeable erect penis. I chuckled when I glanced at it again. The figure was over a foot tall and was exquisitely made. "I'd love to know who all lived in that damned mansion if there were items like this sitting out on display."

Cara frowned. "The old place on the bluff, right?"

"Yeah, why?"

"I forget you didn't grow up around here," she said, leaning against the counter. "Rumor is that Oak Hollow had its own residential cult. Or at least a witch."

"Seriously?" I said, my brow rising.

"Eh, it's just a story, but no one really saw the

lady who lived there. Never had the house serviced for anything. Never came into town to get things. There was a huge garden and orchard around the property, if I recall. Some say on the night of the full moon, you could catch her outside, dancing around a fire. Naked." The way she pronounced it, it was more like nekkid.

I chuckled. "Probably very freeing. The orchard and garden were still there." I remembered seeing the curling, iron fence that had surrounded a massive garden. "The house wasn't in bad shape, come to think of it. They said it was a hundred years old or so."

"Oldest mansion in southern Missouri," she mused. "It's weird, though. I looked it up once. There's no actual date for the place, nor records of it anywhere. It's like the place just appeared one day."

"Spoo-oo-ooky," I teased, wiggling creepy-scary fingers at her.

She flipped me off. "Whatever. I'm going to get the last crate. Lunch break after?"

"Sounds good to me. Want to go dance naked around a fire later?" I said, already turning my gaze to the next item in the box at my feet.

"You think you're so funny," she said, her voice trailing away.

I went back to my work, singing softly under my breath while I jotted down note after note. Three pieces later, including two more interesting statues of naked women, and an intricately sculpted face mask that was a mix between a stag and a devil, Cara flicked on the radio.

I rolled my eyes.

"Get a better singing voice."

I tossed a ball of packing paper at her. The mask caught my attention again.

A flash of another being with horns appeared in my mind's eye.

I stilled.

"Just a mask," I murmured to myself, turning my back on it.

I went back to work while Cara puttered around the store. About eight years ago, I found myself in the small town of Oak Hollow. I'd been broke and trying to pick up random shifts at the local diner and bar. One night, a lady with curly blue hair came into the bar, and we started talking. Her name was Florinda Dale. She was an interesting woman. The local crazy was what everyone called her. I'd been upset at first at the nickname, but out here, it was a compliment—a friendly joke. Everyone loved Florinda. This old antique store used to be hers. She offered me a stable job—more stable than the one at the bar—and I'd been here ever since.

Two years ago, she told me she was retiring. I thought she was shutting down the store when she presented me with the deed and the keys to the building. She'd given me the place to run on my own. She'd told me since she had no kids to pass it on to, it was mine. It was the only time I'd seen that woman tear up. I'd say I was doing pretty good, being a couple of years from thirty and owning my own place. Pretty damned good.

Florinda popped in now and again, whenever she was in town. She spent most of the year traveling the country in her old beat-up camper, sending me postcards every so often. The Hidden Treasure Trove —the name of the antique store, I hadn't changed it —was doing just fine, though.

I paused before picking up another item out of the crate, proudly glancing around the shop. Yup, I hadn't done bad at all.

I'd met Cara during my first few months in town and brought her on when Florinda said she could use an extra set of hands. We'd been friends ever since.

"What are you smiling about?" Cara asked, wiping the dust from her hands with a damp rag.

"Can't I simply smile?" I mused. I hadn't actually realized that I was.

"You can, but it always worries me. You don't do it enough. Not genuinely, at least."

The tinkling of the most annoying bell Cara could have found sounded when the front door opened, saving me from responding to her comment. "Your food has arrived, ladies," a cheery voice called.

Dylan was the owner of the Backroad Bakery in the heart of Oak Hollow. I'd asked him about the name once—it's not like it was actually on a back road. More like main road—and he'd shrugged, saying it was the best he could come up with. Somehow, it stuck. His tall frame ducked under a few wind chimes hanging from the heavy wooden beam running through the center of the sprawling shop. His hair was short, and his dark brown eyes glimmered with mischief, as they usually did.

"What trouble did you get into this morning?" I asked, taking the brown paper bag from him.

"The usual. You know how Alicia is. Might be my bakery, but that woman doesn't let me out of the kitchen to do anything. All I wanted to do was change up the front window display. That was a mistake."

I took the bag, turning toward the opposite counter because it was mostly cleared of clutter.

Cara and Dylan were laughing, but the sound was muffled. Suddenly, my pulse raced, and my knees locked. Shaking, I found myself frozen in place, unable to move or hear a thing except a rushing in my ears. A whimper slipped past my lips. Mentally, I screamed at myself to move beyond it, but my body refused to answer, trapped in a state of intense fear. Chest heaving with my ragged breathing, I sank to the floor in a heap.

Cara and Dylan were there a moment later. Their lips were moving, but I couldn't hear anything. Cara pried the bag from my hand while she situated me on the floor, so my back was against the counter. She took one hand while Dylan held the other, their foreheads creased with worry.

Cara was trying to get me to breathe with her, but flashes of a dark night twelve years ago kept appearing before me.

I winced, hearing that horrible growling all over again. The sensation of claws digging into my upper right arm made me flinch. Another whimper broke free of my mouth. All I wanted to do was curl into a ball and disappear.

Another face appeared in my memories. I

calmed. Shimmering amber eyes filled with confusion and concern held me captive. He reached for me, then there was nothing but darkness.

"Jasmine? Come on, open your eyes, Jas."

"Cara?"

Her heavy sigh was punctuated by a stream of curses. "Been a long time since you had one that bad." Her fingers pressed against my wrist. "Thought we were gonna have to call you an ambulance. Thank goodness your heartrate's going down. Shit, woman."

"I'm fine," I mumbled, mouth feeling sluggish. "Really."

"Whatever you say," Cara replied, not sounding convinced.

I opened my eyes to see her scowling. Dylan hovered over us, the cordless phone clutched in his hand. Cell service in this shop was notorious for being shitty. "I don't need an ambulance. This happens. See? I'm all better." I motioned at myself while I tried to stand. My knees wobbled, and I sank right back to the floor.

Dylan and Cara exchanged a look.

"Don't you dare," I ordered. "Give me the phone right now."

Dylan's lips thinned, but he handed it over. Once

it was safely in my grip, I let them help me to my feet. I managed to stay upright this time, not moving away from the counter.

"Don't you have medication or something?" Dylan asked.

"Tried a bunch. Nothing works," I said, waiting for the last of the terror to fade away as if it hadn't just turned me into a puddle of quivering human limbs. "I'll be good in a few minutes."

Dylan appeared less convinced than Cara was. He held up his hands in surrender when I continued to glare. "Make sure she eats," he told her.

I reminded him I wasn't a child. He waved on his way out the door, with the bell's tinkling announcing his exit.

Cara unpacked the sweet buns Dylan had brought us, as well as the muffins, and two chocolate chip cookies. She plopped it all in front of me with strict instructions to eat. I tried to tell her again I was fine, but she crossed her arms and watched me until I finally took a bite.

I was usually starving after those episodes. When the first one happened over a decade ago, the doctors told me they were panic attacks. I wanted to believe them, but deep down, I knew these moments were something else. Not that it really mattered.

I didn't experience an episode every day. Sometimes I'd go a few months without having one at all. It was a rare moment I saw flashes of the night that messed up my life or that I blacked out entirely.

"You ever going to tell me about what happened?" Cara asked.

"What are you talking about?"

"You never talk about your past, which is fine," she said in a rush. "But you went through something. I know you did, and I just want you to know I'm here for you if you ever want to talk about it." She dropped the pieces of the muffin she'd torn apart, not eating a thing.

"Why are you asking me that now?" I asked quietly. "You've seen me have fits before."

She shrugged, not meeting my eye. "You were whispering under your breath this time."

"I was?"

She nodded, shoving her food across the counter. When her hazel eyes met my gaze, they were filled with worry. "You said something about a car. Then a... hound? And Dylan said you mentioned the word demon a few times."

I forced a laugh. "Demons? Okay, I think you two have been watching too many of those ghost hunter shows lately."

"Are you sure you're alright?"

"Yeah. I promise. I'm going to get back to work now."

She continued to hover, so I started singing in my off-key voice until she sighed, flipped on the radio, and went back to setting up new displays.

A couple of locals came in, as well as people passing through town. We sold two paintings, a bookshelf, and a rather sizeable old metal plow that had been sitting out front for ages. At five on the dot, I flipped the sign over on the door, announcing we were closed.

"You heading home?" Cara asked, snagging her violet leather purse from under the counter.

"I've got one more crate to go through. I won't be long."

"I can stay."

"I'll see you in the morning," I said, waving her off. "Night."

She grumbled, but the door opened and closed. I went to lock it, pulled the shades on the front windows, turned off the radio, and picked out a vinyl from the shelf, flipped on the turntable I kept behind the counter.

The sound of folksy music filled the shop.

There were only four items left in the crate left to

catalog. Three of them were hand-embroidered items, each showing a different floral scene with black roses and lilies on dark burgundy. Once they were documented, I picked up the narrow wooden black box at the bottom.

"What are you?" I murmured, checking the box for any indication of what was inside.

I knew most of the items that would be in the crates, but this box, I couldn't recall seeing it at the sale the day before. There'd been so much stuff, though, I could've easily overlooked it. Carefully, I flipped open the silver clasp.

"Holy shit," I whispered, glimpsing the knife resting on a black silk bed. No, not a knife. A dagger. The blade was about a foot long, the hilt another eight or so inches on top of that. The sheath covering it was encrusted in red and black stones that glimmered beneath the overhead lights. "Where did you come from?"

Curiosity warred with apprehension until I gave in and picked up the dagger. It was heavy in my grip. There was a chunk of smoky stone at the base of the hilt. I thought it might be smoky quartz. I'd have to call a few of my experts to see what it was. Not to mention with the other stones that decorated the object. Carefully, I tugged the dagger free of the sheath.

The hilt warmed in my hand.

I frowned. "Overtired," I muttered. "You're just overtired. Nothing's changing temperature."

I tried to ignore the sensation, only the heat increased. I yelped a few seconds later, dropping the dagger while I clutched my right hand in my left. The lights flickered at the same time a rush of cold air gusted through the shop. Then everything went back to normal.

Mostly.

Biting back a string of curses, I glared from the dagger to my palm, bright red and stinging. A circle appeared to mark my skin, with a strange, harsh design at the center of it.

I blinked and the image faded.

I stood in that one spot for a solid minute until I managed to get my body to move again. "Maybe you've been watching too many supernatural shows," I grumbled. "You're tired. It was a long day. Just leave it for tomorrow."

By the time I had the dagger packed in the box and was ready to head out, my hand no longer hurt. The redness had faded, too. Brushing it off as my imagination getting carried away, I locked up the shop, climbed into my beat-up old Jeep, and headed home.

The headlights lit up the faded gray farmhouse with its wrap-around front porch. The place needed work when I bought it five years ago. I was slowly making headway. Very slowly. My home was in a constant state of renovation. On the plus side, there was no one around me for a few miles. Just me and the trees. I had a garden of my own but planned to make it larger. Maybe adding a small orchard. I wasn't exactly in a hurry. I didn't plan on leaving Oak Hollow any time soon.

This might not have been the town I was raised in, but it sure as hell felt more like home than home did those last few years.

The porch steps creaked when I stomped up them, the front door also greeting me with a loud squeak. I tossed my keys and purse on the front table, kicked out of my black boots, and trudged to the bedroom. More exhausted than I realized, I barely stepped out of my jeans, got my bra off, and fell onto the bed as my eyes were slipping closed, and I passed out.

"Shit," I yelled, bolting upright in bed what felt like maybe minutes later.

I FUMBLED for the lamp on the nightstand. Soft light flooded the room, and I shoved my messy hair from my face. With a grunt, I flopped back down, wiping the sheen of sweat from my forehead. My body tingled, and I bit my lip, recalling all too vividly the dream I'd had. I'd been in my bedroom, but I hadn't been alone. A tall, broad-shouldered figure had filled the doorway. I hadn't been scared of him. Oh, no. I'd held out my hand for his. He'd growled my name and tumbled into bed with me.

I fisted my hand in the comforter, feeling his heated lips pressing against my neck all over again. His hands, god, his hands had been everywhere. They'd caressed my back, dragging me closer while his tongue had plunged into my mouth, dominating the kiss. He'd ripped my clothes from my body without any effort at all. I scrunched my eyes shut, seeing him slide down my body to bury his face between my legs. I gasped, an unexpected burst of pleasure shooting through me, much as it had in the dream. I'd still been shaking with ecstasy when he'd covered my body with his, whispered my name, and filled me completely. My hand drifted across my stomach to between my legs, unable to resist sating my desires before trying to go back to sleep.

Soaking wet from the dream, I quickly shimmied

out of my black panties, flipped off the lamp, and shed my t-shirt, too. I wasn't a stranger to taking care of myself since I tended to avoid relationships, but I couldn't remember the last time a damned dream had turned me on to this extent.

The man's face remained in shadow, but I felt his firm body pressed against mine. My fingers glided up and down my sex then teased that sweet bundle of nerves. I plunged them inside, mirroring how his body had moved, filling me over and over until I didn't think I could take any more. I cupped my breast, pinching my nipple while my back arched off the bed. My gasp turned into a sharp cry. An echo of his groan of release filled my ears, and I could have sworn, for that moment, he really was there with me, his face pressed to my neck, his warm breath sending a pleasurable chill down my spine.

Breathing heavily, I collapsed to the bed, wishing that dream hadn't been simply a dream. Ready to go back to sleep, I shut my eyes, only to open them again and sit upright, heart pounding.

Shimmering amber eyes. That's what I'd seen in my dream.

Covering my face with my hands, I told myself it meant nothing. So what if I'd been muttering under my breath today while freaking out on the shop floor? Didn't matter. And just because those eyes were the ones I saw after having a mind-blowing sex dream didn't mean he was going to randomly show up. He couldn't. It'd been twelve years. If he was going to burst into my life again, he would've done it by now.

Yanking the comforter over my head, I told myself to just go to sleep. I was fine. Everything was perfectly fine.

CHAPTER 2

ARKON

The sun had set an hour ago, the evening air crisp with the sweet smell of fall rustling through the leaves overhead. I hated it. Lip curling in disgust, I snarled quietly at the surrounding woods that reminded me, day after day, that I still wasn't where I should be.

I threw my head back, glaring at the stars blinking into sight while the crescent moon rose higher into the sky. My brothers had told me to try and find some joy in this world. Some beauty to make me happy. They didn't believe in returning to the underworld. That we'd ever have a chance to go back home. Our real home. Our family had been torn apart, and we were forced to the surface to live among mortals and the creatures who felt the desire to mingle with them.

Not me. The underworld was where I belonged. One way or another, the demon prince who thought he could take it away from me would pay.

I tugged on the ends of my newly acquired black leather jacket, then leaned against a nearby tree. My boots had sunk into the mud a while ago. Each time I moved, they made a squishing sound that was getting on my last nerve.

A snort came from behind me. I glared over my shoulder at the large buck staring me down. He pawed at the ground, grunting louder. A growl rumbled through my chest, and it took off into the brush, its white tail flashing in the shadows. I was no stranger to the woods. Miles of forest was far easier to hide in because I didn't want to use glamour to conceal my true face from the world.

When I wasn't sulking beneath the trees, I'd hit up whatever dive bars I could find in whatever town I happened to be in. For nearly two decades, I'd been fighting to track down a way to pierce the veil that would let me into the underworld. Once there, I could seek my revenge. There was no point in plotting Prince Carridan's death until I could complete that first step.

Constantly dodging bounty hunters sure as Hades didn't exactly make my life any easier.

My brothers and I were supposed to be dead. If a demon ever managed to report that we were, in fact, alive, not only would my life be in danger, but my brothers' lives would, too. They had some semblance of normal lives. I was the one who wasn't able to let go. I was too much like Prince Gorath, our father. He'd always been the warrior. They were too much like our mother, willing to not hold onto grudges that would eventually wear down the soul.

No matter what my brothers told me, it didn't break my resolve to carry out my revenge. If one of us didn't attempt to avenge our father's death, his soul would find a way to come back and haunt us, I was damned sure of it.

Something tickled the beard on my face. I raised my hand, pulling off an orb-weaver spider. It crawled over my fingers, and I turned, gently setting it on the bark of the tree. "They're late," I muttered to the spider, not that it would know what I was saying. "I left a big enough trail for a child to follow. The quality of good bounty hunters appears to be lacking of late."

Earlier that morning, I'd purchased a magical trap from a local witch. One called Cyrene. There'd been several demons trailing me through the woods of Missouri over the last three days. If the rumors I'd been hearing were correct, they were some of Carridan's demons. A majority of the bounty hunters were under his employ. This pair didn't realize they were following me but seemed to think they were trailing another demon on Carridan's kill list. Too bad he was now dead.

I was the one who put him in the ground a week prior. Bastard had snuck up on me outside a bar and tried to knife me. Thought he was going to return to Carridan and be able to plead for his life if he delivered news of having killed me. His death saved me the trouble of trying to lure the hunters to me without revealing who I was. I'd taken the dead demon's leather jacket, a chunk of his hair, his blood, and some skin for good measure, leaving a trail for the others to follow. If I captured them alive, I'd have someone to question about Carridan's movements in the underworld as well as on the surface. With any luck, I'd find a way to use them to get my ass back through the veil.

If I shut my eyes, I could sense the magical doorway leading to the underworld. It was only a few miles south of here, tucked away in the dark of the woods. No one could simply walk through it. If they could, the underworld would be tossing out humans left and right after they'd stupidly stumbled into it. The princes all bore rings granting them access, as did their mates and heirs. Mine and my brothers were taken and destroyed. Other tokens were gifted to bounty hunters, the personal guards of the princes, and any demon who needed to pass through the veil regularly. I'd take whatever tokens these bounty hunters had on them and hand them over to the witch. She'd do her magic and once they were attuned to me, I'd have my way in.

"Easy," I grumbled, knowing it wasn't. Not even close.

Magic always came with a cost. The witch, Cyrene, had asked me if I was ready to pay it when I purchased this trap from her. I'd said yes, and she'd merely looked at me. I'd been using magic for years after my parents realized I had a knack for it. Most demons could manipulate it slightly, which was why most of us could pass as humans in this world. Creating a glamour was the first spell demons learned. I proved to have a bit more talent and thus was trained in secret. I'd been warned a long time ago that using magic always came with a price, no matter the amount of magic used.

Revenge was all that mattered now. I'd pay whatever the price to see it done.

The wind shifted directions, and a new scent caught my attention. I'd left the blood, skin, and hair in the middle of the small grove of cedars. Using glamour, I concealed myself to blend in with the surrounding shadows. Blocking my scent had taken a bit more effort. Cyrene had aided me in that regard, too. I'd downed the potion to keep my scent from being picked up hours ago.

The moment the demons entered the trap, they'd be caught in a magical cage that would last twenty-four hours. Plenty of time to torture information out of them. Relishing the blood about to be spilled, knowing they were of Carridan's line, I reached for the jagged-edged knife sheathed at my hip.

Footsteps crunched over leaves, and the quiet murmur of two, deep male voices echoed around the trees. Thirty more yards, then twenty. I held my breath, not daring to move an inch to give myself away. Not yet.

"Where you at, Borag?" a voice shouted. "Make it easy on all of us, eh? Just come out now."

"He's not going to do that, you dumbass," a second voice replied.

"You never know. Borag never was the brightest demon."

"Just snag him, and let's get out of here. I hate the mud and the bugs."

"You hate everything up here," the first demon replied.

Two shapes loomed out of the darkness a mere ten yards away from me. The trap was right in front of them. A few more feet, and I'd have them in my grasp. I'd thought I'd recognized their voices when they first called out. The moment they stepped into the grove and turned in my direction, I swallowed back a furious snarl.

Jorl and Feral. They'd been there the day my father was killed.

They'd laughed when his head was severed from his body.

"I don't see him," Jorl, the first demon, said, sighing. He sniffed the air, giving his head a shake. "Trail's fresh, though."

Feral shrugged. They entered the grove.

A bright flash of red light blinded me. Their panicked shout followed by furious snarling told me the trap worked. When I could see again, I smirked at the glowing red bars forming a circular cage around the two demons. Drawing the dagger from my side, I stepped out of the shadows, not caring how much noise I made now.

"Who's that?" Jorl snapped while Feral growled ferociously from beside him. They reached for the bars, and the cage struck back, jolting them until they let go.

"Your death," I replied, keeping my voice as emotionless as possible.

Jorl squinted, yelling at Feral to shut up. "You're not Borag."

"Borag's dead. You should worry about yourselves right now," I said, strolling around the cage.

Jorl's shimmering blue eyes followed me. "Is that right?" He touched the bars again, snarling when they shocked him a second time. He sniffed the air, grunting. "You're a demon. Demons don't use magic."

"Depends on the demon."

"So you're a coward," he said, to which I growled. "What do you want, huh? We won't tell you anything."

"We'll see." I raised my blade, ready to open the cage enough to drag half of Jorl through when the breeze that had been steadily blowing died.

A hush fell over the grove. It was like something

sucked the air out of my lungs. I gasped, right along with Jorl and Feral.

A second later, a massive shockwave rolled through the forest, knocking down tree limbs and tearing saplings from the ground. I grunted as my back crashed into a tree trunk, splitting it down the middle. The cage holding Jorl and Feral vanished with a loud popping sound, and they hit the ground in a tangled heap of limbs.

Leaves rained down around me while I pushed to my feet with a groan. Somehow, I managed to keep hold of my dagger. I shook my head, pinching the bridge of my nose at the sharp, stabbing pain behind my eyes. A massive burst of magic was the only explanation for what just happened. There were no witch covens in the vicinity and no magical artifacts that could create such a disturbance, at least as far as I knew. The pulsing magic that remained in the air like a nagging whisper proclaimed otherwise. Whatever it was, it had power. A weapon of some kind? Why was it out here in the middle of nowhere?

"Well now," Feral said, and I stilled at the delight in his voice. "Arkon. You're supposed to be dead."

The glamour, it must've come off when the shockwave hit. Adjusting my grip on the dagger, I planted my feet. Neither of them could leave here alive. I sure as hell couldn't let them beat me to whatever object contained that much power either. If it was a weapon, something with that much strength in it could help me defeat Carridan.

Feral and Jorl split, trying to surround me. Feral laughed like the maniac he was and lunged forward. I ducked under his wild swing in time to avoid Jorl's kick to my side. I sidestepped Jorl's second attack and swiped at his stomach with my dagger.

Jorl sucked in a sharp breath, and blood wet the blade. I smiled, holding it up, but my small victory was short-lived. Feral threw himself at my back, wrapping his arms around my neck.

I slammed him into a tree.

His arm shifted, and I bit deep into the muscles with my fangs. Tearing a chunk of skin and muscle free, I bit down a second time. Howling, he let me go enough to grab hold of him and toss him over my head.

A burning pain made my back arch. I whirled around, catching Jorl in the shoulder with my fist. He had a dagger in each hand now, sneering while he motioned me forward. With Feral holding his wounded arm, spouting curses, I gave all my atten-tion to Jorl. Our blades clashed, the noise bouncing off the trees to come right back to us.

I knocked one of his blades free then smashed my fist into his face repeatedly, forcing him back. He attempted to stab me. I snatched his wrist, and with a vicious twist, broke it. The bone jutted through the skin while he howled, dropping his second blade. With a roar, I buried my knife into his shoulder, pinning him to a tree trunk.

"You," he growled, sucking in air, "you're going to die. Carridan will tear you to pieces."

Not bothering with words, I snarled and dragged my dagger across his neck, cutting him down to his spine. A second strike relieved him of his head, a head I kicked toward Feral, who was finally regaining his feet. He glanced down at the head resting before him.

"For my father," I snapped.

Feral's lip peeled back from his fangs. He let out a howl and threw himself at me like a wild beast. His claws embedded in my right shoulder and twisted. The dagger slipped from my hand in my attempt to stop him from tearing my throat out with his fangs. With one hand on his throat and the other working to get his claws free, I hit the ground, pinning him with my weight. The fall did nothing to jar him loose. His claws sunk in deeper.

I grunted as his razor-sharp canines tore through

skin and muscle, down my arm, and finally came free with a sickening wet sound. Fumbling through the leaves and dirt for a weapon, I struggled to keep Feral pinned. His claws stabbed into my thighs and sides over and over.

Finally, my fingers brushed across something solid. Hefting the rock high, I smashed it into Feral's face. His skull cracked. I hit him until his body went limp. There was nothing left of his face. The rock rolled from my fingers as I slid from his corpse, grimacing at the multitude of wounds covering my body. Blood soaked my clothes. Shrugging out of the ruined leather jacket, I chucked it aside and fell to my back.

"Feral?"

Damn it. Of course there was another one.

"You guys feel that earlier?" the demon shouted. "It's still here, too. Something funky in the air. Stop fucking around so we can figure out what that was. Borag can wait 'til morning. Carridan will be pissed if we don't check this out."

Holding a hand to my side, trying to staunch the worst of the bleeding, I scrambled to my feet. What little strength remained in me I put toward a glamour to hide my face. My scent was all over this place, though. With any luck, Borag's and the others' scents would cover my tracks long enough to give me a head start.

The torn-up Mustang I'd been driving was a few miles from here. Trekking through the woods and managing not to fall off a bluff in the dark didn't sound appealing. I had no other choice but to get my ass moving. I set off into the darkness, moving as fast as I dared. The demon's shouts faded. I let out a brief sigh of relief. He wasn't following me.

Yet.

I picked up the pace, staggering and tripping over tree roots and sticks. A few times, I ran into thorny brambles that only served to add to my irritation and blood loss. The whispering magic in the wind wasn't helping matters.

Three times, I sensed I was going in the wrong direction. After a quick look at the stars, I'd sag in defeat and have to shift until I was headed to the car again.

The fourth time, I gave up trying to resist the pull of magic, too weak to tell my feet to stop.

The sky lightened, and a mad chuckle escaped me. I'd been stumbling around in the dark all night. No idea where I was now, I shut my eyes and blindly followed the trail of magic growing sharper with each step I took. When the sounds of leaves rustling switched to gravel crunching, I sluggishly lifted my eyelids. The magic was strong enough now to make my hair stand on end. The glamour, at least, was still in place. I only knew this because I stood in front of a Jeep and saw my reflection in the window.

Behind the vehicle was a one-story metal building. There were windows to the right of a wooden front door. A sign was close by, but my vision was fuzzy.

How much blood had I lost? The wounds at my shoulder and side were still oozing when I quickly checked them over. I was going to drop any second. My eyes shut, and I swooned, ready to do just that when a force shoved me forward.

The noise that had been more of a sensation against my skin earlier was now a steady hum. The hum turned into a song I was helpless to ignore. At the front door to the building, I reached blindly for a knob. It turned, and the door swung inward.

A horrible bell tinkled overhead, disrupting the hum of magic. I growled, wanting it to stop. There were no lights on inside, but a woman was mumbling under her breath.

"Not open—holy shit!"

I had a half-second to spot the woman with wavy, dark brown hair coming toward me when my legs gave out. Neon blue nails were the next thing I saw, followed by a pair of wide, gray eyes.

I frowned or tried to.

I knew those eyes.

"Hey, stay awake," she commanded, gripping my left shoulder hard. "Can you hear me?"

I grunted in an attempt to answer, then let the darkness take over, lulled to it by the magic pulsing around me.

CHAPTER 3

I pressed my hands to the bleeding wound at the man's shoulder. He was covered in so much blood, I wasn't even sure where to start. Had he been attacked by a bear? We had black bears, but shit, I didn't think they'd do this much damage. Usually, they ran away from people. Mountain lion, maybe?

"Come on," I snapped. "Wake up, damn it. You don't get to come into my store and just pass out. Or die. No doing that either. Damn it. This is not how I saw my Thursday going."

Unable to really go back to sleep after the crazy bout of dreams I had, I'd given up and planned on coming into the shop to finish setting up the new items from yesterday. Only when I came to the shop, none of the lights would come on. The whole place was without power. I'd pulled out my cell to call Cara and see if the town was out, too, but there was no service. Wouldn't you know it. Nothing about this morning was starting out right.

I'd been about to walk up the road a ways to get a signal when a bleeding guy stumbled into my store. This was great. Really. I hadn't even had my coffee yet.

"You need an ambulance," I muttered. "There's no way I can get you to my Jeep."

Not wanting to leave him, but needing to get him help, I debated trying to haul him out the front door anyway. I doubted he'd thank me for dragging his ass over gravel. Then again, after that, I'd still have to get him into my vehicle.

There was no way. No flipping way.

I wasn't weak, not by a long shot, but I sure as hell couldn't deadlift a two-hundred-plus pound man. The nearest person to me was over two miles away. If I left him that long, there was a good chance he might not make it. I had no idea how bad his wounds really were or how many he had.

"Think, Jas, just think," I muttered, playing with the silver spinner ring I wore on my middle finger. The vines and flowers went around and around until

I gave up on being struck by a brilliant idea. Rushing to the back room, I snagged the first aid kit and high-tailed it back to the guy still bleeding on my floor.

Each time I pressed fresh gauze to a different injury, the guy flinched. A few times, I was sure I heard him growl. He never opened his eyes, though his random muttering made me jump more than once. Whatever he was saying, it wasn't English. Some of the wounds looked like punctures.

Gently, I tugged his shredded t-shirt upward, wiping away the blood so I could see the extent of his injuries. I felt the blood drain from my face from examining the number of lacerations. There were even more on his thighs, too.

I was going to run out of gauze and bandaging before I covered them all.

Deciding I'd deal with the worst ones first and hope the rest would be alright until I got him help, I checked his right shoulder. The second I touched the injury, he jerked, his upper lip twitching.

I froze at the sound rumbling in his chest. That was definitely a growl. It had to be. And not any old manly growl. No sir, no how.

That was full beast growling. An echo from an old memory surfaced. I'd heard that sound before.

"Don't," I ordered myself. "You're just freaked out

cause there's a dying man on your floor. And you had that attack yesterday. You're letting your imagination run away with you. Just stop."

He made the noise again.

My gut clenched. Humming loudly to cover the growling, I went back to tending to his shoulder. While I worked, I kept catching a weird shadow passing over his face. A few times, I thought his hair turned black and his skin darkened.

I shook my head to clear it, and then his sandy, messy locks returned. Shrugging it off as adrenaline and shock at having a half-dead man appear on my doorstep, I hummed louder to try and stay calm, telling myself everything was fine.

My head down, examining another deep set of punctures, I picked up the sound of steps on the gravel outside. Hoping it was Cara deciding to come in extremely early for once, I waited until the bell sounded to warn her. "Hey, don't freak out, but we have a situation."

"I can see that," a male voice replied.

I flinched, turning halfway around.

He stood just inside the store, his long, brown jacket hanging to his knees. The t-shirt underneath was black, and his boots were caked with mud and leaves. His brow furrowed in concern when he glanced from me to the bleeding man on my floor.

When his eyes narrowed, a shiver raced down my spine, and I had the strangest urge to put myself between the stranger and the injured man.

"Does your phone have service?" I asked, amazed my voice didn't shake.

"Afraid I don't have a phone."

"Okay, that's fine. Do you think you can help me get him to my Jeep? It's not too far..." I peered around him to the front door when it hit me. "You know, I don't even open for another three hours. Why, uh—why are you here?"

The man's blue eyes shimmered, and when he smiled, a set of fangs hung over his bottom lip. "I simply love antiques," he replied with a growl. "Where is it?"

Unable to look away from the fangs and the way the man's face slowly shifted into that of another, I gulped, shaking my head.

This isn't happening, not again. Oh, hell no. Not again.

"Where's what?" I sidled around the guy on the floor, trying to put myself between him and the thing I was pretty damned sure attacked him.

The man I was sure was a demon.

What was I even thinking? No. I wasn't going back to that dark place. This had to be some messed-up nightmare. Demons weren't real. Giant demonic hounds didn't exist. It was all in my head. I pinched my arm, then winced. When I didn't wake up, fear seized my spine in an icy grip.

Shit. This is bad.

The man bared those fangs then stormed around me and started tearing through the shop. Glass shattered as he knocked things to the floor, the growling turning to furious snarling. "I know it's here," he shouted, tossing a table filled with glassware as if it weighed nothing.

I cringed when it slammed into the wall sending several mirrors to the floor in a mess of glass shards.

"What did you do with it?"

"I don't know what you're talking about," I snapped.

He stomped toward me.

I scrambled to get up—

His hand fisted in my hair, yanking me to my feet.

I screamed at the sharp pain, kicking to get away. His grip tightened. He dragged me to him, his face inches from mine. He opened his mouth wide.

Those wicked fangs had grown longer, a clear threat that he'd easily rip my throat out.

"Tell me, and I'll make your death a quick one."

"I don't know what you're talking about," I whispered, barely able to get the words past my lips.

He rolled his eyes and shook me.

I yelped then I was flying across the room. I slammed onto the top of the counter. My back throbbed. Grimacing, I tried to get up, but the asshat was right back on me, pinning me to the hard surface with one hand flat against my chest. Was he that tall when he walked in? Or his shoulders that broad? My gaze skipped over the face that had changed, too, and I froze at what was now atop his head.

Horns. There were short, twisted horns growing out of his head.

I really effin' hate when I'm right.

His laugh was dark. He dragged black claws down my cheek, his brow arching. "You're lying, but that's alright. I could use some entertainment today. He doesn't look like he'll last long enough for some fun. But you, well, you're fresh meat." His claws pricked my chin, forcing my face to turn back to him. He buried his nose in my hair, and I gagged at the delighted sounds coming from his throat.

The scars on the back of my right arm gave a twinge, and I was back to that night so many years ago. It was the first time I'd seen a creature like this one.

A demon.

I'd been told I was crazy back then. I'd suffered through years of therapy and doctors telling me I was either lying or crazy. Spent more years on medications that did nothing but leave me feeling miserable and like a shell of a person. But the proof that demons were real was currently holding me hostage.

My hands inched along the counter, but there was nothing to grab—no weapon in reach for me to bash the bastard over the head with. Furious tears burned in my eyes. I wasn't going to be killed in my own damned shop by something that shouldn't even exist.

The demon was talking again, but I wasn't listening to how he planned to torture me. If I didn't get rid of him soon, Cara would be walking through that door. It was bad enough I might die. I wasn't about to let my friend bite the dust, too.

Think, Jas, think!

My eyes roamed frantically around the shop. The only guns I had here were antiques. There was no ammo for them, either. I had a metal bat I kept under the counter, but it was about fifteen feet away. The demon's hand roamed down my arm then to my hip, and I kicked on instinct. He laughed at my feeble attempts to make him stop.

"Oh no, sweetheart, you're all mine now," he murmured.

Deciding that landing a lucky strike while struggling was my only chance, I screamed in his face and punched and slapped him as hard as I could. His laughter only served to piss me off even more.

Vaguely, I noted my right palm stinging. Figuring it was from hitting him, I ignored it. The stinging turned into a searing burn. When I screamed this time, it was out of pain. I didn't think I could take anymore when the air was abruptly sucked out of my lungs.

The room spun, and an explosion of heat shot from my hand. The demon snarled, soaring through the air to land on the other end of the shop, taking several shelving units with him.

Something heavy slammed into my hand. I staggered into the counter I slid off of, trying to clear the dizziness from my head.

"The hell?"

Gripped in my palm was the red and black

encrusted dagger I'd discovered last night. How had it gotten here? I wasn't even close to it. The pain in my hand stopped, at least.

"You bitch," the demon bellowed, throwing shelves and furniture out of his way while he stormed back to me. "I'm going to tear you to pieces!"

I had no idea how to use a dagger and wasn't about to try. I tucked it in the back of my jeans and ran for the metal baseball bat instead. That, I knew damned well I could swing. I'd just gotten it in my hands when claws dug into my shoulders and threw me over the counter. I took out a set of chairs on my way to the floor.

Every inch of me aching, I attempted to take a swift mental account of what might be broken. The demon was on me again, hauling me to my feet. He opened his mouth and damn if those fangs didn't look more than ready to rip into my throat when a hand landed on his shoulder.

A hand with long, sharp-looking claws.

The demon attacking me cursed and then was torn away.

I fell to my knees, cringing at the blood soaking the shoulders of my navy blue long-sleeve shirt. Shoving the hair from my face, I lifted my head to see the wounded man now before me. He was a few inches taller, and he too was now broader at the shoulders. The muscles in his arms bulged. Two twisted horns protruded from his head a little behind his hairline, hair that was now black as night but still messy. A beard also covered his face. He glanced at me over his shoulder, and the rest of the world disappeared.

Shimmering amber eyes.

Heat flooded my body, and my cheeks burned. The demon's eyes narrowed a hint then the first demon was charging him.

"Stay out of the way," he snarled and met the attacker head-on.

I ducked to the side, gaze fixed on the demons duking it out in my shop.

Their growls and roars were deafening. I winced each time one of them landed a hit. The one with the amber eyes moved faster than I expected him to after being wounded. It was like he was possessed.

The one trying to kill him was quickly backpedaling.

He said something, but I was too far away to hear it.

Amber Eyes roared, the sound rooting me to the

spot. He grabbed the other demon by his throat and squeezed until there was a loud crack.

I clapped a hand over my mouth, fighting the urge to be sick. Then he proceeded to tear out the demon's throat with his claws. The head toppled free of the limp body that then proceeded to collapse to the floor.

My stomach roiled.

"You," Amber Eyes muttered, turning toward me. "How..." His eyes rolled back in his head, and he hit the floor in my shop for a second time that morning.

The silence was thunderous and pressed in around me.

I swallowed and the sound made me jump.

Demons. I had demons in my store.

Granted, one of them was now dead and without a head, but still, they were demons. Not humans.

I took a step, cursed, and rushed to the trashcan behind the counter. I hadn't eaten anything this morning, thankfully. When the heaving finally stopped, I wiped my mouth on my sleeve and inched my way toward Amber Eyes. He was breathing, and the less severe wounds I hadn't bandaged yet appeared to be better as if they were healing on their own.

Memories flicked through my mind the longer I

stared at his face. Back then, he didn't have a beard or been as ferocious. It was him, though, the same demon who burst into my life long enough to mess it up.

Seized by a spike of anger I'd held in for twelve years, I kicked Amber Eyes in the hip. "Asshole."

He growled but didn't come to.

Tapping my cheeks, I paced madly around the shop, trying to come up with a plan. If I called anyone here to help, they'd either think I was crazy, or they'd end up hurt. The last time I claimed monsters were running around, it didn't turn out so great.

No one could find out about this incident. I'd walk outside until I had service and call Cara. If I could keep her away from the shop and tell her to post online that we'd be closed today, it'd buy me some time. The shop's power was still out after all. It was a valid excuse. I just needed time.

"Time to do what?" I snapped at myself. "Bury a demon and wait for another one to miraculously keep healing himself enough so he can leave?" A mad giggle passed my lips, and I slapped a hand over my mouth hard enough to hurt.

The pain was good. It jarred me from the shock creeping through my body, making me numb.

One step at a time.

Call Cara. I could do that.

Telling Amber Eyes to stay put, though he didn't appear to be going anywhere anytime soon, I hurried back to the counter for my cell phone. The dagger was still tucked at my lower back. I scanned the shop, looking for the best place to hide it.

Once it was out of sight, I ran for the front door. My palm ached like it wanted the dagger back.

"Too much," I whispered under my breath, stepping out into the chilly morning air. "Too damned much. You better not be here to ruin my life a second time," I muttered and started walking until I finally had service on my phone.

Copyright © 2021 by Ava Benton

All rights reserved.

No part of this book may be reproduced in any form or by any electronic or mechanical means, including information storage and retrieval systems, without written permission from the author, except for the use of brief quotations in a book review.

AFTERWORD

Click for more Ava Benton works!

Sign up for the newsletter to be notified of new releases.

Click on link for
Newsletter
or put this in your browser window:
mailerlite.com/webforms/landing/m7a8c5